Georg Manville Fenn

# The Dark House

ℒeseklassiker

Georg Manville Fenn

**The Dark House**

ISBN/EAN: 9783955630713

Auflage: 1

Erscheinungsjahr: 2013

Erscheinungsort: Bremen, Deutschland

# Contents

# Chapter One.
## Number 9A, Albemarle Square.

"Don't drink our sherry, Charles?"

Mr Preenham, the butler, stood by the table in the gloomy servants' hall, as if he had received a shock.

"No, sir; I took 'em up the beer at first, and they shook their heads and asked for wine, and when I took 'em the sherry they shook their heads again, and the one who speaks English said they want key-aunty."

"Well, all I have got to say," exclaimed the portly cook, "is, that if I had known what was going to take place, I wouldn't have stopped an hour after the old man died. It's wicked! And something awful will happen, as sure as my name's Thompson."

"Don't say that, Mrs Thompson," said the mild-looking butler. "It is very dreadful, though."

"Dreadful isn't the word. Are we ancient Egyptians? I declare, ever since them Hightalians have been in the house, going about like three dark conspirators in a play, I've had the creeps. I say, it didn't ought to be allowed."

"What am I to say to them, sir?" said the footman, a strongly built man, with shifty eyes and quickly twitching lips.

"Well, look here, Charles," said the butler, slowly wiping his mouth with his hand, "We have no Chianti wine. You must take them a bottle of Chambertin."

"My!" ejaculated cook.

"Chambertin, sir?"

"It's Mr Girtle's orders. They've come here straight from Paris on purpose, and they are to have everything they want."

The butler left the gloomy room, and Mrs Thompson, a stout lady, who moved only when she was obliged, turned to the thin, elderly housemaid.

"Mark my words, Ann," she said. "It's contr'y to nature, and it'll bring a curse."

"Well," said the woman, "it can't make the house more dull than it has been."

"I don't know," said the cook.

"I never see a house before where there was no need to shut the shutters and pull down the blinds because some one's dead."

"Well, it is a gloomy place, Ann, but we've done all these years most as we liked. One meal a day and the rest at his club, and never any company. There ain't many places like that."

"No," sighed Ann. "I suppose we shall all have to go."

"Oh, I don't know, my dear. Mr Ramo says he thinks master's left all his money his great nephew, Mr Capel, and may be he'll have the house painted up and the rooms cleaned, and keep lots of company. An' he may marry this Miss Dungeon — ain't her name?"

"D'E-n-g-h-i-e-n," said the housemaid, spelling it slowly. "I don't know what you call it. She's very handsome, but so orty. I like Miss Lawrence. Only to think, master never seeing a soul, and living all these years in this great shut-up house, and then, as soon as the breath's out of his body, all these relatives turning up."

"Where the carcase is, there the eagles are gathered together," said cook, solemnly.

"Oh, don't talk like that, cook."

"You're not obliged to listen, my dear," said cook, rubbing her knees gently.

"I declare, it's been grievous to me," continued the housemaid, "all those beautiful rooms, full of splendid furniture, and one not allowed to do more than keep 'em just clean. Not a blind drawn up, or a window opened. It's always been as if there was a funeral in the house. Think master was crossed in love?"

"No. Not he. Mr Ramo said that master was twice over married to great Indian princesses, abroad. I s'pose they left him all their money. Oh, here is Mr Ramo!"

The door had opened, and a tall, thin old Hindoo, with piercing dark eyes and wrinkled brown face, came softly in. He was dressed in a long, dark, red silken cassock, that seemed as if woven in one piece, and fitted his spare form rather closely from neck to heel; a white cloth girdle was tied round his waist, and for sole ornament there were a couple of plain gold rings in his ears.

As he entered he raised his thin, largely-veined brown hands to his closely-cropped head, half making the native salaam, and then, said in good English:

"Mr Preenham not here?"

"He'll be back directly, Mr Ramo," said the cook. "There, there, do sit down, you look worn out."

The Hindoo shook his head and walked to the window, which looked out into an inner area.

At that moment the butler entered, and the Hindoo turned to him quickly, and laid his hand upon his arm.

"There, there, don't fret about it, Mr Ramo," said the butler. "It's what we must all come to — some day."

"Yes, but this, this," said the Hindoo, in a low, excited voice. "Is — is it right?"

The butler was silent for a few moments.

"Well," he said at last, "it's right, and its wrong, as you may say. It's master's own orders, for there it was in his own handwriting in his desk. 'Instructions for my solicitor.' Mr Girtle showed it me, being an old family servant."

"Yes, yes — he showed it to me."

"Oh, it was all there," continued the butler. "Well, as I was saying, it's right so far; but it's wrong, because it's not like a Christian burial."

"No, no," cried the Hindoo, excitedly. "Those men — they make me mad. I cannot bear it. Look!" he cried, "he should have died out in my country, where we would have laid him on sweet scented woods, and baskets of spices and gums, and there, where the sun shines and the palm trees wave, I, his old servant, would have fired the pile, and he would have risen up in the clouds of smoke, and among the pure clear flames of fire, till nothing but the ashes was left. Yes, yes, that would have been his end," he cried, with flashing eyes, as he seemed to mentally picture the scene; "and then thy servant could have died with thee. Oh, Sahib, Sahib, Sahib!"

He clasped his hands together, the fire died from his eyes, which became suffused with tears, and as he uttered the last word thrice in a low moaning voice, he stood rocking himself to and fro.

The two women looked horrified and shuddered, but the piteous grief was magnetic, and in the deep silence that fell they began to sob; while the butler blew his nose softly, coughed, and at last laid his hand upon the old servant's shoulder.

"Shake hands, Mr Ramo," he said huskily. "Fifteen years you and me's been together, and if we haven't hit it as we might, well, it was only natural, me being an Englishman and you almost a black; but it's this as brings us all together, natives and furreners, and all. He was a good master, God bless him! and I'm sorry he's gone."

The old Indian looked up at him half wonderingly for a few moments. Then, taking the extended hand in both of his, he held it for a time, and pressed it to his heart, dropped it, and turned to go.

"Won't you take something, Mr Ramo?"

"No — no!" said the Indian, shaking his head, and he glided softly out of the servants' hall, went silently, in his soft yellow leather slippers, down a long passage and up a flight of stone stairs, to pass through a glass door, and stand in the large gloomy hall, in the middle of one of the marble squares that turned the floor into a vast chess-board, round which the giant pieces seemed to be waiting to commence the game.

For the faint light that came through the thick ground-glass fanlight over the great double doors was diffused among black bronze statues and white marble figures of Greek and Roman knights. In one place, seated meditatively, with hands resting upon the knees, there was an Indian god, seeming to watch the floor. In another, a great Japanese warrior, while towards the bottom of the great winding staircase, whose stone steps were covered with heavy dark carpet, was a marble, that imagination might easily have taken for a queen.

Here and there the panelled walls were ornamented with stands of Indian arms and armour, conical helmets, once worn by Eastern chiefs, with pendent curtains, and suits of chain mail. Blood-thirsty daggers, curved scimitars, spears, clumsy matchlocks, and long straight swords, whose hilt was an iron gauntlet, in which the warrior's fingers were laced as they grasped a handle placed at right angles to the blade, after the fashion of a spade. There were shields, too, and bows and arrows, and

tulwars and kukris, any number of warlike imple-
ments from the East, while beside the statues, the
West had to show some curious chairs, and a full-
length portrait of an Englishman in the prime of life
— a handsome, bold-faced man, in the uniform of
one of John Company's regiments, his helmet in his
hand, and his breast adorned with orders and jewels
of foreign make.

The old Indian servant stood there like one of
the statues, as the dining-room door opened and
three dark, closely-shaven and moustached men, in
black, came out softly, and went silently up the
stairs.

There was something singularly furtive and
strange about them as they followed one another in
silence, all three alike in their dress coats and turned-
down white collars, beneath which was a narrow
strip of ribbon, knotted in front.

They passed on and on up the great winding
stairs, past the drawing-room, from whence came
the low buzz of voices, to a door at the back of the
house, beside a great stained-glass window, whose
weird lights shone down upon a lion-skin rug.

Here the first man stopped for his companions,
to reach his side. Then, whispering a few words to
them, he took a key from his pocket, opened the
door, withdrew the key, and entered the darkened
room, closing and locking the door, as the old Indian
crept softly up, sank upon his knees upon the skin
rug, his hands clasped, his head bent down, and
resting against the panels of the door.

## Chapter Two.
## The Dead Man's Relatives.

"I can tell you very little, Mr Capel. I have been your great uncle's confidential solicitor ever since he returned from India. I was a mere boy when he went away. He knew me then, and when he came back he sought me out."

"And that is twenty-five years ago, Mr Girtle?"

"Yes. The year you were born."

"And he made you his confidant?"

"Yes; he gave me his confidence, as far as I think he gave it to any man."

"And did he always live in this way?"

"Always. He filled up the house with the vast collection of curiosities and things that he had been sending home for years, and I expected that he would entertain, and lead the life of an English gentleman; but no, the house has been closed for twenty-five years."

Mr Girtle, a clean-shaven old gentleman, with yellow face, dark, restless eyes and bright grey hair, took a pinch of snuff from a handsome gold box, flicked a few grains from his white shirt-front, and said "Hah."

"Had my uncle met with any great disappointment?" said the first speaker, a frank-looking man with closely curling brown hair, and a high, white forehead.

"What, to make him take to this strange life? Oh, no. He was peculiar, but not unhappy. He liked to be alone, but he was always bright and cheerful at his club."

"You met him there, then?" said a fresh voice, and a handsome, dark young fellow, who had been leaning back in an easy chair in the dim drawing-room, sat up quickly, playing with his little black moustache.

"Oh, yes! I used to dine with Colonel Capel when we had business to transact."

"But, here you say he led the life of a miser!" continued the young man, crossing his legs, and examining the toe of his patent leather boot.

"I beg your pardon, Mr Gerard Artis, I did not say that. Your great uncle was no miser. He spent money freely, sometimes, in charities. Yes," he continued, turning to where two ladies were seated. "Colonel Capel was often very charitable."

"I never saw his name in any charitable list," said the darker of the two ladies, speaking in a sweet, silvery voice; and her beautiful regular features seemed to attract both the previous speakers.

"No, Miss D'Enghien, I suppose not," said the old man, nodding his head and rising to begin walking up and down, snuff-box in hand. "Neither did I. But he was very charitable in his own particular way, and he was very kind."

"Yes," said the young man who had first spoken; "very kind. I have him to thank for my school and college education."

"Well — yes," said the old lawyer; "I suppose it is no breach of confidence to say that it is so."

"And I have to thank him for mine, and the pleasant life I have led, Mr Girtle, have I not?" said the second of the ladies; and, but for the gloom, the flush that came into her sweet face would have been plainly visible.

At that moment the footman entered with a letter upon a massive salver, and as he walked straight to the old lawyer, he cast quick, furtive glances at the other occupants of the room.

"A note, eh?" said the old solicitor, balancing his gold-rimmed glasses upon his nose; "um — um — yes, exactly — very delicate of them to write. Tell them I will see them shortly, Charles."

The footman bowed, and was retiring as silently as he came over the soft carpet, when he was checked by the old solicitor.

"You will tell Mr Preenham to see that these gentlemen have every attention."

"Yes sir."

The footman left the room almost without a sound, for the door was opened and closed noiselessly. The only thing that broke the terrible silence that seemed to reign was the faint clink of the silver tray against one of the metal buttons of the man's coat. As for the magnificently furnished room, with its heavy curtains and drawn-down blinds, it seemed to have grown darker, so that the faint gleams of light that had hung in a dull way on the faces of the great mirrors and the gilded carving of console and cheffonier, had died out. It required no great effort of the imagination to believe that the influence of the dead man who had passed so many solitary years in that shut-up house was still among them, making itself felt with a weight from which they could not free themselves.

Paul Capel looked across at the beautiful face of Katrine D'Enghien, thinking of her creole extraction, and the half French, half American father who had married his relative. He expected to see her looking agitated as her cousin, Lydia Lawrence, but she sat back with one arm gracefully hanging over the side of the chair, her lustrous eyes half closed; and a pang strongly akin to jealousy shot through him as it seemed that those eyes were resting on the young elegant at his side.

"Yes," said the old solicitor, suddenly, and his voice made all start but Miss D'Enghien, who did not even move her eyelids; "as I was saying," he went on, tapping his snuff-box, "I can tell you very little, Mr Capel, until the will is read."

"Then there is a will?" said Miss D'Enghien.

The old lawyer's brows wrinkled, as he glanced at her in surprise.

"Yes, my dear young lady, there is a will."

"And it will be read, of course, directly after the funeral?" said the dark young man.

The lawyer did not reply.

"I suppose you think it's bad form of a man asking such questions now; but really, Mr Girtle, it would be worse form for a fellow to be pulling a long face about one he never saw."

"But he was your father's friend."

"Oh, yes, of course."

"Hence you, sir, are here," continued the lawyer. "My instructions were clear enough. I was to invite you here at this painful time, and take my old friend's place as your host."

"You have been most kind, Mr Girtle," said Miss D'Enghien.

"I thank you, madam, and I grieve that you should have to be present at so painful a time. My next instructions were to send for the Italian professor, who is here to carry out the wishes of the deceased."

"Horrible idea for a man to wish to be embalmed," said Artis, brutally.

Lydia Lawrence shuddered, and turned away her face. Paul Capel glanced indignantly at the speaker, and then turned to gaze at Katrine D'Enghien, who sat perfectly unmoved, her hand still hanging from the side of the chair, as if to show the graceful contour of her arm.

"Colonel Capel had been a great part of his life in the East, Mr Artis," said the old lawyer, coldly. "He had had the matter in his mind for some time."

"How do you know that?"

"By the date on my instructions, which also contained the Italian professor's card."

"And I suppose we shall have a very eccentric will, sir."

"Yes," said the lawyer quietly, "a very eccentric will."

"Come, that's refreshing," said the young man with a fidgetty movement. "Well, you are not very communicative, Mr Girtle. You family solicitors are as close as your deed boxes."

"Yes," said the old lawyer, closing his gold snuff-box with a loud snap.

"Well, come, it can be no breach of confidence to tell us when the funeral is to be?"

The old lawyer took a turn or two up and down the room, snuff-box in hand, the bright metal glistening as he swung his hand to and fro. Then he stopped short, and said slowly:

"The successor to Colonel Capel's enormous property will inherit under extremely peculiar conditions, duly set forth in the will it will be my duty to read to you."

"After the funeral?" said Gerard Artis.

"No, sir; there will be no funeral."

"No funeral!" exclaimed Artis and Paul Capel in a breath, and then they rose to their feet, startled more than they would have cared to own, for at that moment a strange wild cry seemed to come from the staircase, followed by a heavy crash.

"Good Heavens!" cried the old lawyer, dropping his snuff-box.

Katrine D'Enghien alone remained unmoved, with her head turned towards the door.

# Chapter Three.
## One Guardian of the Treasure.

Paul Capel was the first to recover from the surprise, and to hurry from the darkened room, followed by Artis and the late Colonel's solicitor, though it was into no blaze of light, for the staircase was equally gloomy.

The source of the strange noise was not far to seek, for, as they reached the landing, they became aware that a fierce struggle was going on in the direction of the room occupied by the late Colonel, and hurrying there, it was to find two men locked together, one of whom was succeeding in holding the other down, and wresting his neck from the sinewy hands which had torn off his white cravat.

"Why, Charles! Ramo!" exclaimed Mr Girtle, in the midst of the hoarse, panting sounds uttered by the contending men.

"He's mad!" cried the former, in a high-pitched tone, in which a man's rage was mingled with a schoolboy's whimpering fear. "He's mad, sir. He tried to strangle me."

"Thief! dog!" panted the old Hindoo, with his dark features convulsed with passion. "Wanted — rob — his master!"

The two young men had separated the combatants, who now stood up, the footman, his vest and shirt torn open, and his coat dragged half off — the old man with one sleeve of his dark silk robe gone, and the back rent to the waist, while there was a fierce, vindictive look in his working features, as he had to be held to keep him from closing with the footman again.

"What does this mean, Charles?" cried Mr Girtle, as the butler and the other servants came hurrying up, while the three Italians also stood upon the landing, looking wonderingly on.

"If you please, sir, I don't know," said the footman, in an ill-used tone. "I was just going by the Colonel's door, and I thought, as was very natural, that I should like to see what these gentlemen had done, when Mr Ramo sprang at me like a wild cat."

"No, no!" cried the old Indian, whose English in his rage and excitement was less distinct, "a thief — come to rob — my dear lord — a thief!"

"I hope, sir," said the footman, growing calmer and looking in an injured way at Mr Girtle, "you know me better than that, sir. Mr Preenham here will tell you I've cleaned the plate regular all the ten years I've been here."

The old solicitor turned to the butler.

"Yes, sir; Charles's duty has been to clean the plate, but it is in my charge, and I have kept the strictest account of it. A little disposed to show temper, sometimes, sir, but strictly honest and very clean."

"This is a very sad and unseemly business at such a time," said Mr Girtle. "Ramo, you have made a mistake."

"No, no!" cried the old Indian, wrathfully.

"Come, come," said Mr Girtle; "be reasonable."

"The police," panted the old Indian. "Send for the police."

"All right," cried Charles, defiantly; "send for the police and let 'em search me."

"Silence!" cried Mr Girtle. "Go down and arrange your dress, sir. Mr Capel, young ladies, will you return to the drawing-room? Signori, will you retire? That will do, Preenham. Leave Ramo to me."

In another minute the old solicitor was left with Ramo, who stood beneath the dim stained-glass window, with his arms folded and his brow knit.

"You do not trust and believe me, sir?"

"Don't talk nonsense, Ramo. You know I trust you as the most faithful fellow in the world."

He held out his hand as he spoke, but the old Indian remained motionless for the moment; then, seizing the hand extended to him, he bent over it, holding it to his breast.

"My dear lord's old friend," he said.

"That's better, Ramo," said Mr Girtle. "Now, go and change your dress."

"No, no!" cried the old man. "I must watch."

"Nonsense, man. Don't think that every one who comes means to rob."

"But I do," cried the old Indian, in a whisper. "They think of what we know — you and I only. Those foreign men — the servants."

"You must not be so suspicious, Ramo. It will be all right."

"It will not be all right, Sahib," cried the old Indian. "Think of what there is in yonder."

"But we have the secret, Ramo."

"Yes — yes; but suppose there were others who knew the secret — who had heard of it. Sahib, I will be faithful to the dead."

The old Indian drew himself up with dignity, and took his place once more before the door.

"It has been shocking," whispered the Indian. "I have been driven away, while those foreign men did what they pleased in there. It was maddening. Ah!"

He clapped his hands to his head.

"What now, Ramo?"

"Those three men! Suppose — "

He caught at his companion's arm, whispered a few words, and they entered the darkened room, from which, as the door opened and closed, a peculiar aromatic odour floated out.

As the door was closed the sound of a bolt being shot inside was heard, and directly after the face of Charles, the footman, appeared from the gloom below. He came up the stairs rapidly, glanced round and stepped softly to the closed door, where he bent down, listening.

As he stood in the recess the gloom was so great that he was almost invisible, save his face, while just beyond him a large group in bronze, of a club-armed centaur, seemed to have the crouching man as part of the artist's design, the centaur being, apparently, about to strike him down, while, to give realism to the scene, a dull red glow from the stained-glass window fell across his forehead.

As he listened there, his ear to the key-hole and his eyes watchfully wandering up and down the staircase, a dull and smothered clang was heard as if in the distance, like the closing of some heavy iron door. Then there was a louder sound, with a quick, short report, as if a powerful spring had been set in motion and shot home. Then a door seemed to be closed and locked, and the man glided quickly over the soft, thick carpet — melting away, as it were, in the gloom.

The door opened and, from the darkness within, Mr Girtle and the old Indian stepped slowly out, bringing with them a soft, warm puff of the aromatic odour, and, as they grew more distinct in the faint light of the stained-glass window, everything was so still in the great house that there was a strange unreality about them, fostered by the silence of their tread.

"There, now you are satisfied," said the old lawyer, gently. "Go and change your robe."

The Indian shook his head.

"I will stay till your return inside the room."

"Inside?" said the Indian.

"Yes — why not? You and I have reached the

time of life when death has ceased to have terrors. He is only taking the sleep that comes to all."

There was a gentle sadness in the lawyer's voice, and then, turning the handle of the door, he opened it and stood looking back.

"You will not be long," he said. "They are waiting for me in the drawing-room."

The door closed just as the old Indian made a step forward to follow. Then he stood with his hands clenched and eyes starting listening intently, while the centaur's club seemed to be quivering in the gloom, ready to crush him down.

The old man raised his hand to the door — let it fall — raised it again — let it fall — turned to go — started back — and then, as if fighting hard with himself, he turned once more, and with an activity not to be expected in one of his years, bounded up the staircase and disappeared.

Ten minutes had not elapsed before he seemed to come silently out of the gloom again, and was half-way to the door, when there was a faint creak from below, as if from a rusty hinge.

The old man stopped short, crouching down by the balustrade, listening, his eyes shining in the dim twilight; but no other sound was heard, and he rose quickly, ran softly down, and with trembling hands opened the door.

Mr Girtle came slowly out, looking sad and depressed, and laid his hand upon the Indian's shoulder.

"You mean to watch, then," he said.

The Indian nodded quickly, his eyes gazing searchingly at the lawyer the while.

"Are you going in, or here?"

"My place was at the Sahib's door."

"Good!" said the solicitor, bowing his head; and he returned to the drawing-room, Ramo watching him suspiciously till the door closed.

As he stood there, the dusky tint of the robe he now wore seemed to lend itself to the surrounding gloom, being almost invisible against the portal, as he remained there with his fingers nervously quivering, and his face drawn by the agitation of his breast.

He shook his head violently the next moment, clasped his hands together, and sank down once more upon the lion-skin mat, bent to the very floor, more like some rounded mass than a human being: while the great centaur was indistinctly seen, with his raised club, as if about to repeat the blow that had crushed the old Indian into a motionless heap.

# Chapter Four.
## The Lawyer's Tin Box.

"This has been a terrible week, Katrine," said Lydia Lawrence, taking her cousin's hand.

"Do you think so?"

"Oh, yes. I have not your *sang froid*. I would give anything to go back to the country."

"I have been curious to know all about the will. That old man has been maddening. He might have spoken."

"But his instructions, clear. The will was to be read after he had lain there a week."

"Lain in state," said Katrine, with a curl of her lip. "With a savage crouching on a lion-skin at his door like some dog. Pah! It is absurd. More like a scent in a French play than a bit of nineteenth century life."

Lydia sighed.

"I felt greatly relieved when those dreadful men had gone."

"What, the Italian professors? Pooh! what a child you are. I did not mind."

Lydia gazed at her with a feeling of shrinking wonder, and there was something almost fierce in the beautiful eyes, as Katrine sat there by one of the tables of the ill-lit drawing-room, the two pairs of wax candles in old-fashioned silver sticks seeming to emit but a feeble light, and but for the warm glow of the fire, the great room would have been sombre in the extreme.

"What time is it, Lydia? There, don't start like that. What a kitten you are."

"You spoke so suddenly, dear. It is half-past ten."

"Only half-past ten. Nearly an hour and a half before the play begins. I wish we had kept the tea things."

"Pray don't speak so lightly, Katrine."

"I can't help it. It is so absurd for the old man to have left instructions for all this meretricious romance to surround his end. As for old Girtle, he seems to delight in it, and goes about the house rubbing his hands like an undertaker."

"Katrine!"

"Well, he does. Will read at half-past eleven at night on the tenth day after the old man's death. It is absurd. Ah, well, I suppose a millionaire has a right to be eccentric, if he likes."

"Dear Katrine, he was always so good."

"Good! Bah! What did he ever do for me? He hated my branch of the family, and our Creole blood. As if the D'Enghiens were not a fine old French family before the Capels were heard of."

"But Katrine — "

"I will speak. I was dragged here to be present at this mummery, to have for my share a hundred pounds to buy mourning, and I vow I'll spend it in Chinese mourning, and wear yellow instead of black. Why don't those men come up instead of sitting smoking in that dining-room and leaving us alone in this mausoleum of a place? Here, ring, and send for them; I'm getting nervous, too. I'm catching it from you — weak little baby that you are."

At that moment the door opened, and the two young men entered to go up to them, both speaking to Lydia, and then drawing their chairs nearer to Katrine.

"Are you nearly ready for the play, Mr Capel?" she said, after a time.

"The play!" he exclaimed.

"Yes; the curtain will rise directly. How do you feel, Gerard?"

"Oh, I don't know. I want to hear how many chips the old boy has left me. Deuced glad to get out of this tomb. I say, would you mind me lighting a cigar?"

"I don't mind," said Katrine, lightly.

"Would you mind, Miss Lawrence?"

"Mind — your smoking — here?" said Lydia hastily. "I — I don't think I should, but — "

"No, no," said Capel; "it is impossible. For heaven's sake, pay a little respect to the ladies, if you cannot to the dead."

Artis started to his feet.

"Look here, Paul Capel," he cried angrily; "you have taken upon yourself several times since I have been locked-up here with you to use confoundedly offensive language to me. How dare you speak to me like that?"

"Dare?" cried Capel, rising. "Pooh!" he ejaculated, throwing himself back, and glancing at Katrine, whose eyes seemed to flash with eager pleasure, while Lydia half rose, with extended hands; "I am forgetting myself."

Lydia sank back with a sigh, while Katrine's eyes flashed, and her lip curled.

"Forgetting yourself!" cried Artis. "By Jove, sir, you've done nothing else! I suppose you expect to have all the old man's money, but we shall see."

"Don't be alarmed, Miss Lawrence," said Capel, smiling. "I am not going to quarrel. Ah, here is Mr Girtle."

The door opened, and Charles entered, with two more lighted candles, one in each hand, preceding Mr Girtle, who came in bearing a large tin deed box. This he slowly proceeded to place upon the carpet beside a small table, on which Charles deposited the candlesticks.

"I think I am punctual," said the lawyer, taking his old gold watch from his fob, and replacing it with a nod. "Yes, nearly half-past eleven. Charles, will you summon all the servants. I think everyone is mentioned in the will," he added, as Charles left the room. "You will excuse all formalities. I am strictly obeying instructions as to time and place."

25

The old gentleman took a jingling bunch of keys from his pocket, bent down and opened the tin box, from which he took out a square folded parchment, crossed with broad green ribbons, and bearing a great seal.

This he laid upon the table before him, and sinking back in his chair, proceeded to deliberately take snuff. A dead silence reigned, and, in spite of himself, Paul Capel felt agitated, and sought from time to time to catch Katrine's eye; while Lydia looked from one to the other sadly, and Gerard Artis lay back in his chair.

The door once more opened, and the servants filed in, led by Preenham, the butler, Ramo coming last, to stand with his arms folded and his head bent down upon his chest.

"Be seated," said Mr Girtle; and his voice sounded solemn and strange.

There was a rustling as the servants sat down in a row near the door, Ramo doubling his legs beneath him, and crouching on the floor.

"The last will and testament of John Arthur Capel, late Colonel in the Honourable East India Company's Service, Special Commissioner with her Highness the Ranee of Illahad; Resident at the court of her Highness the Begum of Rahahbad!"

So read the confidential solicitor and friend of the deceased, in a husky voice, his gold-rimmed glasses helping him to decipher the brown writing or endorsement of the yellow parchment. Then he continued: —

"I have followed out the instructions of the deceased to the letter, so far; and now, in continuance of these instructions, in your presence, I proceed to break this seal."

## Chapter Five.
## The Reading of the Will.

There was a peculiar rustle in the gloomy room, a faint sound as of catching of the breath, and above all the sharp crackle of the broken wax as the seal was demolished, and the green ribbon thrown aside.

Then after a prefatory *Hem*! the old lawyer proceeded to read the will, which was in the customary form, and began with a series of bequests to the old and faithful servants of the house, in respect of whose services, and so that there should be no jealous feeling as to amounts, he left each the sum of five hundred pounds free of duty, and ten pounds to each to buy mourning.

"To my old and faithful servant, companion, and friend," — read on the solicitor — "Ramo Ali Jee, two hundred and fifty pounds per annum for the rest of his natural life; the same to be secured in Three-per-cent Consols, reverting at his death as hereinafter stated."

Ramo did not move or utter a word.

"To my old friend and adviser, Joshua Girtle, of the Inner Temple, the plain gold signet ring on the fourth finger of my left hand."

Then followed a few more minor bequests, and instructions of a very simple nature, ending one long paragraph in the will; and as Mr Girtle removed his glasses, and proceeded deliberately to wipe them, the servants took advantage of the gloom where they sat to give each other a congratulatory shake of the hand.

"I now come to the important bequests," said Mr Girtle, rebalancing his glasses in his calm deliberate way.

"To Katrine Leveillée D'Enghien, daughter of my niece, Harriet D'Enghien, formerly Capel, the gold bangle presented to me by the Ranee, and one hundred pounds, free of duty, to buy mourning."

"There, what did I tell you?" said Katrine, in a low, sweet voice, as she smiled at her companions.

"To Gerard Artis, son of my cousin, William Artis," read on Mr Girtle, in the same monotonous, unmoved way; and then he stopped to draw one of the candles forward in front of the parchment.

The young man shifted his position uneasily, and drew in his breath quickly as he thought of the testator's immense wealth, and glanced at Katrine.

"I shall not get all," he thought, "for he will leave something to Paul Capel."

Then, after what seemed an age of suspense, the old solicitor went on:

"The sum of one hundred pounds, free of duty, to buy mourning."

There was a death-like stillness as the lawyer paused.

"Go on, sir, go on," cried Artis, in a harsh voice.

"To Lydia Alicia — "

"No, no, finish the bequest to me."

"I did, sir. One hundred pounds to buy mourning."

"What? Treat me worse than his servants?"

"I believe, Mr Artis, if you will excuse me, that a testator has a perfect right to do what he likes with his own."

"Then you influenced him," cried Artis furiously. "I shall dispute the will."

The old gentleman smiled.

"Influenced my old friend to leave me his signet ring, eh, Mr Artis? No, sir, the will was written by Colonel Capel himself, and afterwards transferred to parchment. If you will allow me. I will proceed."

"I shall dispute the will. I say so at once," cried Artis, "that there may be no mistake. One hundred pounds each to Miss D'Enghien and myself! It is absurd, paltry, pitiful."

"You never saw the testator, Mr Artis?"

"No, sir."

"Neither did you, Miss D'Enghien?"

"I? Oh no."

"He told me himself," continued the old lawyer, "that he had never seen either Miss Lawrence or Mr Paul Capel."

Lydia murmured an assent.

"No," said Capel, who felt a curious oppression at the chest, "I never saw my great uncle. I never even heard from or wrote to him."

"May I ask why?"

"I knew he was reported to be immensely rich, and — well, I felt that he might think I was trying to curry favour."

"Let me see, Mr Artis, I think the deceased did pay your debts?"

"Is this meant for an insult, sir?"

"No, sir; it was a business-like defence of my old friend's memory. To proceed: —

"To Lydia Alicia Lawrence, my grand-niece, twenty-five thousand pounds, free of duty, the same to be invested in Consols, and if she marries, to be secured by marriage settlements to herself and children."

There was a buzz of congratulation here, as the old solicitor once more wiped his glasses and arranged them and the candles, while, in spite of his endeavours to preserve his calmness, Paul Capel, the only one present yet unmentioned, felt the oppression increasing, and the air in the great gloomy room seemed to have become thick and hard to breathe.

He was as if in a dream as the lawyer went on:

"To Paul Capel, son of my nephew, Paul Capel, I leave my freehold house and furniture, library, plate, pictures, statues, bronzes, and curios, conditionally that the house be kept during his lifetime in the same state as it is in now.

"Conditionally, also, that my body, after embalming, according to my instructions, be carried into the room leading out of my bedroom, and placed in the iron receptacle I had specially constructed, without religious rite or ceremony of any kind. I have tried to make my peace with my Creator; to Him I leave the rest. This done, the iron chamber to be locked in the presence of the said Paul Capel, who shall take the key. The doorway shall then be built-up with blocks of stone similar to those of which I had the room built, a sufficiency of which are stored up in cellar Number 4, sealed with my seal.

"And I here solemnly bind my heir and successor to observe exactly these my commands, that my body may rest undisturbed in my old home, under penalty of forfeiture of the said freehold as above named."

"He must have been mad," said Artis, in an audible voice.

"And as I, being now in full possession of my senses," continued Mr Girtle, slightly raising his voice, "know that this is a strange and arduous burden to lay upon my heir in chief, though I have taken such precautions that in a short time my presence in the house may entirely be forgotten, I give and bequeath to him for his sole use and enjoyment — and in the hope that with the help and advice of my old friend, Joshua Girtle, he will sensibly invest, and sell and invest — the Russian leather case containing Bank of England notes amounting to five hundred thousand pounds."

Artis drew a long breath through his teeth; Katrine D'Enghien leaned forward, with her beautiful eyes fixed on Paul Capel; Lydia sank back in her seat with a feeling of misery she could not have explained seeming to crush her; while Paul Capel sat now unmoved.

"And," continued the old lawyer, "the flat silver case containing the diamonds, pearls, rubies, and emeralds, bequeathed to me by my mistresses, the Ranee of Illahad and Begum of Rahahbad, valued at one million sterling, more or less. These cases are in the steel chest in the iron chamber in which my coffin is to be placed when the cases are taken out, the keys of which, and the secret of the lock, being known only to my old friend, Joshua Girtle, whom I constitute my sole executor, and my old friend and servant, Ramo, whom I commend to the care of my grand-nephew, the said Paul Capel.

"Furthermore, the remainder of the sum of fifty thousand pounds in Consols, after providing for the payments hereinbefore stated as legacies, I desire my executor to distribute in twenty equal sums to as many deserving charities as he may select."

The reading of the rest of the document occupied scarcely a couple of minutes, and then the old solicitor rose. The servants slowly left the room, making a détour so as to bow and courtesy to the Colonel's heir, Ramo last — furtively watching Charles — to go slowly to the young man's side, bow reverently, take his hand, and kiss it, saying softly the one word:

"Sahib."

"Don't go, Ramo," said Mr Girtle; and the old Indian slowly backed into the corner by the door, where he stood nearly invisible, waiting until such time as he should be called upon to give up his share of the secret of the chamber beyond the dead man's room.

# Chapter Six.
## A Fit of Generosity.

"Mr Paul Capel," said the old solicitor, "allow me to add my congratulations, and my hope that your fortune may prove a blessing."

"But it is like a dream — a romance," cried Paul Capel. "All that wealth here — in this house! I wonder that he was not robbed."

"My old friend took great precautions against that," said Mr Girtle. "As you will see, it was impossible for any one to have stolen the valuables and notes."

"But ought not this money to have been banked?"

"Of course — or invested. I have told him so, often; but he used to say he preferred to keep it as it was. He had plenty for his wants and charities. Your uncle was an eccentric man, Mr Capel; there is no denying that."

"Eccentric!" cried Artis. "Mad. Well, I give you all warning. I shall take action, and throw it into chancery."

He walked to the end of the room, and Paul Capel looked after him uneasily as he saw Katrine follow.

"You foolish boy!" she whispered; "am not I as badly used as you? Be patient. Wait."

"What do you mean?" he whispered, hastily.

She looked full in his eyes, and he tried to read the mystery in their depths, but without avail.

"Why don't you speak?" he cried.

"Some things are better left unspoken," she replied. "Don't be rash."

"I'll wait." he whispered, "if you wish it."

"I do wish it. Take no notice of what I say or do. Promise me that."

"Promise me you will not make me jealous, and I'll wait."

"But maybe I shall make you jealous," she said. "Still, you know me. Wait."

"I'm sorry for one thing, Mr Girtle," said Paul Capel, while this was going on.

"May I ask what that is?"

"Oh, yes. Your simple bequest of a ring. Will you — you will not be offended, Mr Girtle — out of this immense wealth allow me to make you some suitable — "

"Stop," said the old gentleman, laying his hand upon the speaker's arm. "My old friend wished to leave me a large sum, but I chose that ring in preference. Thank you all the same, my dear young friend, and I beg you will count upon me for help."

"Well, then, there is something I should like to do at once. Look here, Mr Girtle — a million and a half — "

"With its strange burden."

"Oh, I don't mind that. I want to do something over this money. Miss Lawrence is well provided for, but Miss D'Enghien — "

"Well, you had better marry her."

"Do — do you mean that?"

"No," said the old man, sternly; "I do not."

"There is Mr Artis, too. I should like — "

"To find him in funds to carry on a legal war against you for what he would call his rights. My dear Mr Capel, may I, as lawyer, give you a bit of advice?"

"Certainly; I ask it of you."

"Then wait."

Capel drew back as the old gentleman proceeded to fold the will and lay it with other papers in the tin box, while Ramo, standing alone in the gloom, with folded arms and apparently seeing nothing, but observing every motion, hearing almost every word, noticed that Gerard Artis was watching the deposition of the will, his hungry looks seeming to devour it as he felt that he would like to destroy it on the spot.

Ramo noted, too, that Paul Capel took a step or two towards where Katrine was talking eagerly to Artis. Then he hesitated and turned off to where Lydia sat alone.

She, too, had been watching Paul Capel's actions, and now that he turned to her she seemed to shrink back in her seat, as if his coming troubled her.

"Let me congratulate you, Mr Capel," she said, rather coldly.

"Thank you," he said with a sigh; and she saw him glance in the direction of Katrine.

"I think," said Mr Girtle, loudly, "that we will now proceed to fulfil the next part of my instructions."

There was a sharp click heard here, as he locked a little padlock on the tin box, and Gerard Artis watched him, thinking what a little there was between him and the obnoxious will.

"Miss D'Enghien, Miss Lawrence, will you kindly follow me? Ramo, lead the way."

It was like going from one gloom into another far deeper, as the door was thrown open, and Ramo led the way along the short, wide passage, bearing a silver candlestick, whose light played softly on the great stained window when he stopped, and illuminated the bronze club of the centaur, still raised to strike.

The eyes of Gerard Artis were fixed upon the tin box containing the will — the keen look of Katrine D'Enghien on the old Indian servant, as he took a key from his cummerbund — while Paul Capel gazed, with his soul in his glance, on Katrine, ignorant that, with spirit sinking lower and lower, Lydia was watching him.

The solicitor gave a glance around full of solemnity and awe, as if to ask were all ready. Then, as if satisfied, he made a sign to Ramo.

The Indian raised the candlestick above his head, softly thrust in the key, turned it, and threw open the door, when once more, from the darkness within, the strange aromatic odour floated forth.

"Mr Capel, you are master here," said the old lawyer softly. "Enter first."

## Chapter Seven.
## Lying in State.

Paul Capel looked round at Katrine, who gave him a sympathetic glance, and entered the room, taking a step forward and pausing for the rest to follow. Ramo closed the door, and drew a heavy curtain across, whose rings made a peculiar thrilling noise on the thick brass rod.

Ramo then lit two wax candles upon the chimney-piece, and a couple more upon the dressing-table, whose united light was only sufficient to show in a dim way the extent of the room, with its old-fashioned bed and hangings of dark cloth, similar curtains being over the window, and across what seemed to be a second door opposite the couch.

There was an intense desire to look towards the bed, but it was mastered by a strange shrinking, and the visitors to the death-chamber occupied themselves first in looking round at the objects that met their eye.

It was richly furnished, and on every hand it seemed that its occupant had taken precautions to guard himself from the cold of England, after a long sojourn in a hotter land. A thick Turkey carpet was on the floor, large skin rugs were by the fire-place and bedside, dressing-table, and wash-stand. Similar rugs were thrown over the easy-chairs, and on the comfortable couch by the ample fire-place, while here and there were trophies of foreign arms; peculiarly-shaped weapons lay on the dressing-table, and formed the ornamentation of the chimney-piece.

In one corner of the room, carefully arranged and hung upon a stand, was a strangely grotesque object, that, in the semi-darkness, somewhat resembled a human figure, but proved to be the tarnished uniform worn by the old officer — coatee, helmet, sword and belts gorgeous with ornamentation, a pair of pistols with silver butts, and a small flag of faded silk and gilt stuff were grouped over a gold embroidered saddle and tarnished shabrack of Indian work.

Here, too, was one of the Indian figures of Buddha crouched upon an enormous bracket at this side of the room, looking in the obscurity like a living watcher of the dead, in an attitude of contemplation or prayer.

Ramo stood in the silent room, holding the silver candlestick above his head, motionless as another statue, so much in keeping was he in his garb and colour with the surroundings.

But he was keenly watching every one the while, and, taking his cue from a mute question addressed by Mr Girtle's eyes to Paul Capel, he walked solemnly to the head of the heavily hung bed, softly drew back one curtain, and held the candle over his dead master's mortal remains.

Paul Capel felt a natural instinctive shrinking from approaching the bed, but he did not hesitate, stepping forward with reverence, and even then his heart gave a throb of satisfaction that one of his female companions should have stepped calmly to his side.

Lying there as in a darkened tent, with a couple of Indian tulwars crossed upon the bed's head, was a perfectly plain oaken coffin of unusual size, and without the slightest ornamentation save that on the lid, resting against the side, was a brass breastplate bearing the dead man's name, age, and the date of death.

Within — wrapped in a rich robe of Indian fabric, glittering with flowers wrought in gold thread — lay the Colonel, his face visible, and presenting to those who gazed upon it for the first time, the fine features of the old soldier, with his closely cut grey hair, ample beard, and the scars of two sword cuts across brow and cheek.

There was no distortion. The old man, full of days, lay calmly asleep, and Paul Capel bent down and kissed the icy brow.

When he rose his companion pressed forward, and, as he gave way, imitated his action, when, to his surprise, he saw that it was not Katrine D'Enghien, but Lydia.

A low sigh fell upon their ears as they were leaving the bed's head, and Paul raised his eyes to see that the old Indian was watching, and in the semi-darkness he saw him quickly raise a portion of Lydia's dress and hold it to his lips.

Drawing back, they gave place to Katrine and Gerard Artis, who walked to the bed's head, stood for a moment or two, and then, as if moved by the same impulse, both drew away. The old Indian stepped back with his candlestick, the polished silver of which seemed to glimmer and flash in the gloom, the heavy curtain fell in its funereal folds, and the group turned to Mr Girtle.

The old man said a few words to Ramo, who crossed the room to the dressing-table, taking one by one the candlesticks, and placing them in Paul and Lydia's hands, after which he took those from the chimney-piece to give to Katrine and Gerard Artis, the old lawyer taking the one the Indian had carried.

This done, Ramo walked softly to the curtain that covered what seemed to be the second door, and again there was the thrilling sound as the rings swept with a low rattle over the rod, laying bare a strong iron door deep down in a narrow arched portal.

Opening his silken robe, he drew out three keys of curious shape, attached to a stout steel chain which seemed to be round his waist, and softly placing one of them in the lock he turned it easily, when a series of bolts shot back with a loud clang. Then taking out the key, he pressed the door with his shoulder, and it swung slowly and heavily open, apparently requiring all the old man's strength to throw it back.

"Iron, and of great thickness," said Mr Girtle, in a low voice. "Mr Capel, shall I lead the way?"

The Colonel's heir bowed, and, candle in hand, the old lawyer passed through the doorway, Ramo holding back the curtain, and standing like the guardian of the place.

They saw Mr Girtle take a couple of steps forward, turn sharply, and descend, and as Paul Capel followed, he found that to his left were half a dozen broad stone stairs, flanked by a heavy balustrade, and that the old lawyer was standing below, holding up his light.

The next minute, as they reached the floor of what seemed to be a good-sized chamber, there was the sound of the curtain being drawn as if to shut them in, and Ramo came softly down the little flight of steps, to stand at a distance, with reverent mien.

By the light of the five candles they now saw that they were in a perfectly bare-walled chamber, apparently floor, walls, and groined roof of stone, while in the centre stood a large massive cube of solid iron, painted thickly to resemble stone.

So large was it that it seemed as if the remainder of the chamber, left uncovered, merely formed a passage to walk about the four sides.

"This place the Colonel had constructed where a dressing room used to be," said Mr Girtle; and his voice sounded peculiar, being repeated in whispers from the wall in a hollow, metallic ring that was oppressive as it was strange.

"Why the place is like a vault with a tomb in it," said Artis, with an impatient tone in his voice.

"It is a vault, Mr Artis," said the old lawyer — "a vault in which is a tomb. This," he continued, "is all of enormous strength, blocks of stone and concrete being beneath us, and the walls and roof are of immense thickness. The space to be blocked up is six feet through."

"Humph, highly interesting, Mr Showman," muttered Artis; and then, at a look from Katrine, he became attentive.

"Colonel Capel," continued the old lawyer, "had his own peculiar ideas, and being an enormously wealthy man, accustomed to command, he considered he had a right to follow out his views. I more than once pointed out to him, when he made me his confidant, that the proceedings he proposed might meet with opposition from the authorities, but he replied calmly that the place was his own freehold, and that everything was to be carried out privately, but at the same time he would give as little excuse as possible for interference with his plans. Besides, he said, once get the matter over, and it would be forgotten in a week."

"But, in the name of common sense," broke out Artis, "why — "

"Will you kindly retain your observations, Mr Artis, until we have returned to the drawing-room," said the lawyer.

Artis was about to reply, but Paul Capel saw that a look from Katrine restrained him, and a jealous pang shot through his heart.

Balm came for the wound directly, as Katrine raised her eyes to his, let them rest there for a few moments, and then veiled them as she gazed upon the floor.

"Colonel Capel," continued the old lawyer, with his words whispering about the stone walls, "had a double intention in having the place constructed. It was for his mausoleum after death, for his strong room during life. Within this iron room or chamber, which would defy any burglar's tools, is a chest of steel, constructed from the Colonel's own designs, to contain his enormous fortune, and when that has been taken out at twelve o'clock to-morrow, it is to be replaced by the coffin that lies in the next room, by us who are present now; to be closed up and locked; the iron chamber is to be also closed; then the iron door; and lastly, we are to see that portal completely walled up, as I have already told you, and — forgotten."

"But," said Artis, quickly, "is the large sum in notes here — in this place?"

"Yes, sir."

"And the diamonds — the pearls?" said Katrine.

"Yes, my dear young lady, all are here."

"And you have the keys?"

"I and Ramo, the deceased's trusted servant."

"But is — "

Artis was about to continue, "it safe to trust that man?" but, as he spoke, he glanced at Ramo, who was watching him.

"My guide is the series of rules written by Colonel Capel, sir," said Mr Girtle, coldly.

"Can we see the jewels?" said Katrine.

"Yes; you can show us the treasure," cried Artis,

with a half-laugh. "As we two are to have nothing, we might be indulged with a peep."

"The treasure is Mr Paul Capel's, sir," said the old lawyer; "but, even if he expressed a wish, I could not depart from my instructions. To-morrow, at noon, I bid you all to meet me at the door of Colonel Capel's room."

"To-morrow?" said Artis. "To-day."

The old lawyer glanced at his watch.

"Yes," he said, "to-day. I had forgotten that it was so late. Will you kindly accompany me to the drawing-room?"

The Indian went first and drew back the curtain, and they passed up into the bedroom, where the old officer lay in state.

There they paused, as Ramo drew back the iron door and turned the key, when the bolts shot into their sockets, and the curtain was drawn.

Then, glancing at the bed, they passed out of the room, Ramo locking the door, listening sharply, with his ears twitching, as he caught a faint creaking noise made by a lock in the lower part of the house.

"How strange that bronze figure looks," said Mr Girtle, glancing up at the great centaur looming indistinctly against the stained-glass window, in whose recess it stood.

"Yes," said Paul. "It is a fine work, but it looks as if it were going to dash out some one's brains."

"That is what I have always thought whenever I

have entered or left that room."

"I wish to Heaven it had — both of you," muttered Artis. "A hundred pounds. Good God! A hundred pounds!"

The same thought may have entered Katrine D'Enghien's head, for, as they moved towards the drawing-room, she laid her arm affectionately round Lydia's slight waist, and said softly to herself:

"A bangle and a hundred pounds! *Mon Dieu!*"

Then the drawing-room door closed, and Ramo stood in the dark, leaning over the balustrade of the great well staircase, listening intently till he saw a door open, and a flash of light came out, shining on the round, full face of the old butler, and the keen features of Charles, the footman, the latter bearing a tray of silver chamber candlesticks.

Ramo glided away, and the two servants bore the tray to the drawing-room, asked if they would be wanted again, and retired.

"Good-night, dearest," cried Katrine, kissing Lydia affectionately. "I congratulate you. I am not jealous. Good-night, Mr Girtle — how tired you must be," she said, shaking hands. "Good-night, Mr Artis. Good-night, Mr Capel. I congratulate you heartily. Good-night!"

Five minutes later the great drawing-room was as still as the chamber of the dead, and in the dark house — on staircase and in hall — statue and picture looked on, and the kneeling idols crouched with their eyes closed to what was passing, while the great bronze centaur stood with uplifted club, ready to strike there, where he seemed to be on guard, at his dead master's door.

But he struck no blow, and the night passed, and the morning came — a dull, drizzling morning — when the fog hung low, and it was still like night when Preenham, the butler, knocked heavily at Mr Girtle's door.

The old lawyer drew the wire, and the night latch allowed the butler to rush in.

"Hot water, Preenham?" said the old man.

"For Heaven's sake, get up, sir, and I'll call Mr Capel, sir!" panted the butler.

"What! Something wrong?"

"Yes, sir — quick! I'm afraid there's murder done."

# Chapter Eight.
# The Horrors of a Morn.

By the time Mr Girtle was partly dressed and had hurried out on the landing, Paul Capel and Gerard Artis had left their rooms, ready to question him upon the cause of the alarm.

"I don't know," he said, trembling. "Preenham came and roused me — speaking of murder — and, bless my soul! I did not know you were there. Miss Lawrence, too!"

Katrine and Lydia had joined them there on the landing of the second floor, where a chamber candlestick on a table was almost the only light, for that which came through the ground-glass at the top of the staircase was so much yellow gloom.

"One of the maids — Anne — came and woke me," said Katrine, speaking very calmly, as she looked from one to the other, the most collected of any one present. "She said there was something wrong."

"She woke me, too," cried Lydia, who was trembling visibly, and looked of a sallow grey.

"Mr Girtle, will you come down?"

It was the butler's voice, and Paul Capel ran quickly down the stairs to the drawing-room floor, where the old butler, ghastly pale, with his hair sticking to his forehead, had lit half-a-dozen candles and stood them, some on a table, some on the pedestal of the great bronze group outside Colonel Capel's door.

"What is it? Speak, man!" cried Capel.

"The ladies! Don't let the ladies come!"

It was too late; they were already there; and the women-servants were dimly seen in the gloom at the foot of the stairs.

"But what is wrong?" cried Capel.

"I — I — "

The butler passed his hand over his humid face, and looked piteously from one to the other.

"Preenham! Speak, man! At once!" said Mr Girtle, sternly.

"I woke at half-past seven, sir," he said, in a trembling voice, "and wondered that I had not been called at seven. Mr Ramo, sir, always rose very early, and called me and Charles; but I was not surprised, for since master's death, he has slept outside his door, I think — I'm almost sure, though I never said anything to — "

"Man, you are torturing us!" cried Capel.

"Give him time," said Artis, who looked nervous and strange.

"Yes, let him speak," said Katrine. "Go on, Mr Preenham, and tell us."

"Thank you ma'am, I will," said the butler; "but — but would you ladies go back to your room or the drawing-room, I've something — something — "

"I'm not a child," said Katrine. "Lydia, dear, you had better go."

"I will stay with you," said Lydia, laying her hand upon Katrine's arm; and after a helpless look round, and a motion of his hands, as if he washed them of any trouble that might come, the old butler went on.

"I didn't take much notice, as we were late last night, but as soon as I was dressed, I knocked at Charles' door — he sleeps in a turn-up bedstead in the servants' hall."

The old man directed this piece of information to those around him, and then went on.

"There was no answer, so I went in, and Charles was not there."

"Not there?" said Mr Girtle, quickly.

"No, sir. The bed had not been slept in. His livery was on the chair by it, and his cupboard was open where he keeps his private clothes."

"This is strange," said Mr Girtle. "Go on."

"Yes, sir. I thought perhaps he had let himself out through the area gate, sir. He has done such things before, and at a time like this I must speak plain."

"Yes. Let me have the truth. Go on."

"I was very angry, sir, and I meant to tell you, for it seemed disgraceful at such a time."

"Go on."

"I will, sir," faltered the butler, "but you must not flurry me. I have had a shock."

"Let him go on his own way, Mr Capel," said the old lawyer.

Preenham gave him a grateful look and continued:

"I thought I'd go and speak to Mr Ramo, and then I met Cook and Anne."

"We were on the mat, Mr Preenham," said a husky voice from below.

"Yes, Mrs Thompson, quite right, and they went on to the kitchen while I went up into the hall, and undid the bolts of the front hall door, and let down the chain."

"Yes — exactly."

"Then I went up, sir, to see if Mr Ramo was at master's door."

"Yes; go on," said Capel, excitedly.

"And when I came to the door, sir, I found it was ajar, and though I listened, I could not hear a sound. So I pushed the door against the big curtain, and called softly, 'Ramo! Mr Ramo!' but there was no answer, and then I felt a bit alarmed, and, after waiting a moment, I went down and got a light."

"Well?"

"I called again, sir, twice; and then, pushing open the door, a puff of wind nearly blew out the light."

"Wind?" cried Mr Girtle; and he took a step towards the door.

"Stop a minute, sir, please," said the butler appealingly. "I went in quickly, and the first thing I saw was the curtain dragged aside and the window open."

"Yes — go on," cried Mr Girtle, for the butler was trembling so that he could hardly speak.

"And the next, sir — I nearly fell over him — there was poor Mr Ramo — lying — in — a pool of blood."

"Oh!"

The cry came from Lydia as she tottered and clung to Katrine, calm amidst the horrors of the recital.

"I put the candle on the floor, sir, and went down on my knee beside him," cried the butler, growing more and more agitated. "Look," he said, piteously, pointing to his trousers and his hands. "I touched him, sir, but he was dead, sir, dead, and I came up then and alarmed the house."

Artis looked at the butler narrowly, as his eyes wandered from one to the other.

"Have you been in since, Preenham?"

"No, sir. I went and got the candles, and lit all I could."

Capel was about to rush into the room, but he stopped on the threshold.

"Miss D'Enghien — Miss Lawrence — this is no place for you. Pray go back to your rooms."

"Yes," said Katrine, slowly, "Mr Capel is right. Come, dear, with me."

She passed her arm round Lydia, and the two seemed to fade away into the darkness, as Capel, Mr Girtle, Artis, and, lastly, the butler went into the room.

## Chapter Nine.
## Another Discovery.

It was precisely as the butler had said. There was the window open — a window looking out on to some leads. And beyond them the low houses of a mews which ran at the back. There, at a short distance from the bed, was the Colonel's faithful servant, in a pool of blood, with a kukri — one of those ugly curved Indian knives — clasped tightly in his hand.

"Dead!" said Mr Girtle; and then, rising quickly, he ran to the further portal, drew back the curtain, and found the iron door closed.

"There has been a terrible struggle here," said Capel. "Look."

He pointed to where, plainly seen on the white counterpane that half covered the heavy valance, there was the mark of a bloody hand that had caught the quilt and dragged it a little down.

"Yes," said Mr Girtle, looking about at overturned chairs, a small table driven out of its place, and a carriage clock swept off and lying on the floor. "Yes, there has been a terrible struggle."

He looked at the dead man, and then in the direction of the strong chamber.

Artis saw, and said maliciously:

"Murder must mean robbery."

"Impossible!" said the lawyer. "The door is shut. Stop. Let me see," and stooping, he thrust his hand inside the silken robe the old Indian wore.

There was a dead silence as he searched hastily, and then drew out the keys and chain.

"All safe," he cried; "see, here are the keys. They slip off and on this spring swivel; the old man always wore them there. The key of that door; the key of the iron chamber; the key of the steel chest. Gentlemen, I shall remove the keys. Mr Capel, they are yours, now. Take them."

"No," said Capel quietly. "Keep them, sir. Now, what do you make of this? It seems to me that the murderer must have come in by this door, and encountered Ramo, and, after the terrible struggle, have escaped by the window."

"Exactly," said Mr Girtle.

"Unless," said Artis, "some one killed this black fellow when trying to rob his master."

"Absurd!" cried Capel angrily, as he bent down over the dead man. "Look here," he cried, "whoever it was must have been wounded. This knife is covered with blood."

"His own, perhaps," said Artis.

"May be so, but I think not. Now, Mr Girtle, what next?"

"The police," said the old lawyer huskily. "Preenham, fetch me a little brandy; this terrible scene has made me faint."

"Go, sir? Leave you here?"

"Yes, go at once," said Mr Girtle, and there seemed to be an unwillingness to leave, as the butler went out and closed the door.

"You did not want that brandy," said Artis quickly. "You wanted to get rid of him for a few minutes. I know what you are thinking — that it was that scoundrelly-faced footman."

"Yes, you have guessed my thoughts."

"And you suspect the butler?"

"I do not say that, sir," said the lawyer coldly. "We do not know that there has been any robbery until the plate is examined, but we ought to have sent for a doctor at once."

"I'll go," said Capel, and hurrying out of the room, he ran down the stairs, caught his hat from the stand, and hurried from street to street till he saw the familiar red-eyed lamp.

Five minutes after he was on his way back in a cab, with a keen-looking, youngish man, to whom he gave an account of the morning's discovery.

"Have you given notice to the police?"

"No."

"If I were you, I should send a messenger straight to Scotland Yard. It will save you from the blundering of some young constable. Humph — too late."

For, as they reached the room, there was the familiar helmet of one of the force, the man having found the door left open by Capel and rung.

He was a heavy, dull-looking man, who seemed, as he stood in the darkened room, to consider it his duty to thrust his hand in his belt, and stare at the ghastly figure on the floor.

Meanwhile the doctor was busily examining the body of the Indian servant.

"Quite dead!" said Mr Girtle.

"Yes. *Rigor mortis* has set in."

"Suicide?"

"Suicide, sir? Oh, bless my soul, no."

"But that weapon?"

"Yes, some one had an awful cut with that, I should say," continued the doctor, and the constable mentally drew a line from the kukri to the open window, out on to the leads, and down into the mews.

"What has caused his death?"

"I cannot tell you yet," said the doctor. "Hold the light here, closer, please. Hah, that is the mark of a blow on the arm. There is this wound on the chin, and on the neck. Hah! Yes, this seems more likely. There has been a tremendous blow dealt here on the head — but no fracture, I think — sort of blow a life-preserver would give; but, really, I cannot account so far for his death. Unless — What is this peculiar odour?"

"I told you," said Capel, pointing to the bed.

"No, I don't mean that," said the doctor quickly.

"I mean this about here. Can you see any bottle?"

He ran his hand down the side of the silk robe, and then looked round where he knelt.

"What do you mean, doctor?" said Mr Girtle.

"There is the same odour that I should expect to notice in a case of suicide with poison."

"Doesn't look much like that," said Artis. "Why, doctor, look at the traces of the struggle."

"I have looked at them, sir," replied the doctor; "but, so far, I detect no cause for death. A proper examination may give different results, but I must have the assistance of a colleague."

"Done, sir? Finished?" said the constable, who had remained for the time unnoticed.

"Yes, my man. You will give notice of this at once, and lock up the room."

"All in good time, sir. I should like a look round. Door open, you say?"

"Yes," said Mr Girtle.

"Window open?"

"Yes."

"Well, then, the fellow who did it seems to have come in here and escaped there, after getting a cut with that crooked knife."

He turned on his bull's-eye lantern, and made the light play from where the body lay, over the Turkey carpet, to the window, where he turned off the light, for there was sufficient for him to see and examine the seat and sill.

No stains — no marks of hands on the window, no footmarks outside on the leads — not a spot.

He shook his head, and came back.

"Well, my man?" said Mr Girtle.

"Don't be in a hurry, sir. Law moves slow and sure. I was in the country before I got out of the rural into the metropolitan."

"What has that to do with this?" cried Artis.

"Everything, sir," said the constable, turning sharply on the young man, and watching him narrowly. "I've known cases where windows have been set open to make it seem that some one's gone through."

"But the murderer is not in the house," said Mr Girtle, uneasily; "and we suspect — "

"Who's that?" said the constable, sharply. "Oh, you, Mr Butler."

"Yes; I've brought the brandy for Mr Girtle, sir."

"Never mind, now," said the policeman. "Set it down. Gentlemen, I've got a theory about this here."

He turned on his bull's-eye again, as he spoke.

"A theory?" cried Capel, impatiently.

"Yes, sir. You see that crooked knife thing?"

"Yes."

"And the mark of the bloody hand on the counterpane, where it is dragged?"

"Yes, we saw that."

"Well, has any one looked under the bed?"

"No."

"Then we shall find him there."

He stepped forward and raised the heavy valance, directing the light beneath.

"There!" he exclaimed. "What did I say?"

## Chapter Ten.
## "Why, Doctor, he's dead!"

In one moment the slow, heavy-looking constable changed, from a rustic, loutish fellow, to a man full of intelligent observation, for, as he raised the valance of the bed, there, indistinctly seen, was the body of a man, either through fear or to escape observation.

With a quick motion of the hand, the constable opened the leather case at his side, and drew his truncheon.

"Stand at the window, sir," he said to Capel. "You, sir, keep the door. Now, then," he cried, as soon as he had been obeyed, and in a sharp, authoritative voice. "The game's up. Out you came."

Capel set his teeth hard, for all this was horrible in that chamber of death.

"Do you hear?" cried the constable, sharply, for there was neither word nor movement from beneath the bed. "Oh, very well," he continued, "only I warn you I stand no nonsense." And the occupants of the room prepared for a struggle, with beating hearts.

The constable stepped back to them, and from behind his hand, said, softly:

"Be ready, perhaps there's two."

He stepped back and stooped with his staff ready for a blow.

"Now, then," he cried; "is it surrender?"

There was no answer, and, he thrust his hand beneath the bed, seized the man's leg, and dragged him out into the room, but only to loose his hold and start away.

"Why, doctor!" he cried, "he's dead."

The doctor caught up a candlestick and dropped on one knee beside the fresh horror, while the light from the bull's-eye was again brought to bear, and mingled with the wan, yellow rays that struggled in through the panes.

"Good God, gentlemen!" gasped the butler, "it's Charles."

The horribly distorted features were, indeed, those of the footman, and the mystery of the death-chamber began to grow lighter, for it was evident that for some reason he had entered the room in the night. For no good mission, certainly, a short whale-bone-handled life-preserver hanging by a twisted thong from his wrist.

The hideous stains upon the kukri were clearly enough explained by the sight of a terrible gash in the man's throat, and one of his hands was crimsoned and smeared — the one that had left its print upon the quilt, as, in his death struggle, he had rolled beneath the bed.

"No one else there, gentleman," said the constable, looking beneath the bed and making his lantern play there and about the curtains, whilst as it shed its keen light across the calm, sleeping face of the Colonel, the man involuntarily took off his helmet and stepped back on tiptoe.

"Dead some hours," said the doctor, rising.

"It is clear enough," said Mr Girtle, in the midst of the painful silence. "This poor Hindoo was the faithful old servant of my deceased friend, and he died in defence of his master's property."

"Yes, yes," cried the old butler, excitedly. "Charles used to talk about master's money and diamonds in the servants' hall. I used to reprove him, and say that talking about such things was tempting yourself."

"Never asked you to be in it, of course?" said the constable, going close up to him.

"Oh, no; never, sir; but are you quite sure both him and Mr Ramo are dead?"

"Quite," said the constable. "There, you can say what you like, but it's my duty to tell you that I shall take down anything you say, and it may be used in evidence against you."

"Against me!" cried the butler.

"Yes, against you."

But there was no occasion for the note-book, for Preenham closed his lips and did not speak again.

"I think I will satisfy myself, constable, that all is safe here," said Mr Girtle. "Gentlemen, will you come with me?"

He crossed the room, drew back the curtain over the portal and, taking out his keys, unlocked and pushed back the door, descending with the others into the vault-like chamber and examining the massive iron structure in the middle.

"It is quite safe," he said, as the constable made the light of his lantern play here and there.

"But you have not looked in the safe," said Artis, quickly.

"There is no need, sir. No one could have opened it, even with the keys, but Ramo or myself. Nothing has been touched."

The policeman drew a long breath and they returned to the death-chamber, Mr Girtle carefully locking the iron door.

"I don't think we shall want any detectives here, gentlemen," said the constable; "I shall stay on the premises, but perhaps you will let the butler — no, I think one of you, perhaps — will be good enough to send in the first constable you see."

"I am going back," said the doctor. "I can do no more now, policeman. I will send a man to you."

"Thankye, sir, if you will."

"Of course you will give notice to the coroner, and there will be a post-mortem?"

"You leave that to me, sir; only send me one of our men."

They were stealing out on tiptoe, when Capel went back and drew the heavy curtains right across the bed, to shut from the old warrior the horrors that lay in the middle of the room. The constable, too, stepped softly across to fasten the window. Then, following the others out, he closed and locked the door, turning round directly, ducking down, and involuntarily attempting to draw his truncheon, as he raised his left arm to ward off a blow.

"Bah!" he ejaculated. "Why, it's a stature. Looked just as if it was going to knock one down."

# Chapter Eleven.
## The Treasure.

A week of horror and anxiety, during which the customary legal processes had been gone through.

A jury had visited the Dark House and been conducted through the two rooms, to go away disappointed at not seeing the inside of the great iron safe. Then, after the evidence had been given, by the various witnesses at the inquest, including that of the two doctors who had performed the post-mortem examination, a verdict was returned which charged Charles Pillar with willful murder, and stated that the Indian had committed justifiable homicide.

The doctors had differed, as it is proverbially said that they will, Dr Heston, the young medical man, who had been called in first, telling the jury that he was not satisfied that the blows given had caused the death, and drawing attention to the peculiar odour he had noticed. But the Coroner, an old medical man, sided with the colleague, who pooh-poohed the idea, and the verdict was given.

The coroner was a good deal exercised in his mind whether some proceedings ought not to have been taken in respect to the remains of the late Colonel, but he obtained no legal support, and the terrible murder and attempted robbery at Number 9A, Albemarle Square, with the history of the embalming, and the mysterious inner chamber, were public property for the usual nine days, when something fresh occurred, and the interest died away.

Then, once more, there was the old peace in the Dark House, where the remains of Colonel Capel lay in state in the mystery-haunted room.

The servants were very reticent, and consequently but little was heard of the proceedings in Albemarle Square. A good many loiterers had stopped to stare at the darkened windows of the great mansion; but as two coffins had been borne from the place, it was forgotten outside that another still remained. What might have been some busybody's business, became no one's, and the horrible tragedy tended towards the simplification, of the dead man's instructions.

"It is nine days now since the Colonel's commands should have been fulfilled," said Mr Girtle, as they were seated at lunch in the darkened dining-room — the same party, for Katrine had expressed her determination to stay in the house through all the trouble, and Lydia had offered to remain with her.

Katrine and Lydia had kept a great deal to their rooms; Mr Girtle spent most of his time in the library, busy over papers, only appearing at meal times, and, consequently, Paul Capel was thrown a great deal into the society of Gerard Artis, treating him always in the most friendly way, and declining to notice the barbs of the verbal arrows the other was fond of launching.

One of Artis's favourite allusions was to the house his companion inherited.

"I felt horribly jealous of you at first," he said.

"Seemed such a pot of money; but with special commands to live here with a haunted room, and a mausoleum beyond it — no, thank you."

"What shall you do with the chamber of horrors?" said Artis, on another occasion.

"You heard — it is to be built-up."

"No, no; I mean the bedroom. Ugh!"

"I shall take that as my own."

"What? A room haunted with the spirits of three dead men! Bah! Impossible."

Then came the ninth day, and Mr Girtle announced that on the next his instructions should be carried out precisely at twelve.

"That will give you ample time, Mr Capel, to visit a banker afterwards; for, after the late experience, I should not lose an hour in depositing your great uncle's bequest in the hands of your banker."

"You will go with me, I hope."

The old man looked pleased, and nodded.

"But I had reckoned upon seeing the jewels," said Katrine, with a smile at the young heir, which made his heart throb, and Lydia shrink.

"That pleasure must be deferred, Miss D'Enghien," said the old lawyer, crustily; and no more was said.

At twelve o'clock punctually, the next day, Mr Girtle unlocked the door of the Colonel's room, and fulfilling Ramo's duty, held it back while the young men bore in lights; Katrine and Lydia followed, and the old butler, looking shrunken and depressed, came last, to close the door and draw the curtain.

It was mid-day, but it might have been mid-night. Candles were lit again on chimney-piece and dressing-table, and after the old solicitor had seen that the door was fastened within, he took out his key, drew the portal curtain at the end, and then unlocked and slowly pushed open the iron door.

At a given order the butler solemnly carried a couple of candles down into the vault, and stood there in the gloomy stone chamber, where, to those who stood waiting his return, they seemed to cast a peculiarly weird light.

Then, in utter silence, the lid was placed over the calm, sleeping features, and the four men, taking each a handle, lifted and bore the coffin down. There was some little difficulty in the sharp turn of the steps, but in a few minutes all was done, and the coffin lay upon the flagstones, while the two girls stood hand clasping hand.

Mr Girtle walked round to the back of the iron safe and stooped down, when a peculiar clang was heard, as if a spring had been set free, and a large panel at the end where Capel was standing, dropped down.

As the old lawyer came back, candle in hand, it was now seen that the panel that had fallen laid bare a key-hole.

Upon the key being inserted in this, and turned, the panel flew back, and glided over the key-hole as soon as the key was drawn out, displaying a second key-hole, crossed by a row of lettered brass slides.

These the old lawyer manipulated till the letters formed in a row a particular word, when the second key-hole was laid bare, the key inserted and turned, and one end of the iron safe revolved on a pair of huge pivots, shewing the interior — plain, rectangular and dark, with an oblong mass of black metal in the centre.

"The steel chest," said the old lawyer, in a whisper, as he stepped inside the great safe, in which he could nearly stand upright.

Candle in hand he went to the other end, put down the light for a moment to set his hands free to get a second key — a curiously long, thin key, with the end of which he pushed something at the back of the chest. Then, going to one side, he repeated the act, went back round to the other side, and again repeated it, after which he came to the front, and as he held down the light, those who were intently watching his actions saw that there was a small circle of Roman figures, with a hand like that of a small clock, which he pushed round with the end of the key, till it was at the letter V. This done, he bent over the chest, and repeated the action twice upon the top.

Then, as he stepped out, a sharp sound was heard, and a key-hole was laid bare once more. In this he placed the key, turned it, and the steel chest seemed to split open from end to end, dividing in equal parts, which slowly turned over on massive hinges, leaving the centre — a space large enough to hold the coffin — wide open.

"Mr Capel," said the old lawyer, stepping aside, "the next duty is yours. There lie the bank notes and the case of precious stones. I give them over to your care."

Paul Capel hesitated for a moment, glanced at his companions, then back at the opening leading to the Colonel's room, where Katrine and Lydia were watching.

The young man's heart beat heavily as he took the candle, and, stooping down, entered the iron chamber to take from its hiding place his enormous fortune.

It was but a step, and he had only to stretch out his hand to pick up the two cases, but —

The steel chest held nothing.

*The treasure was not there.*

## Chapter Twelve.
## The End of the Instructions.

Paul Capel did not realise his position. "Is there some mistake, Mr Girtle?"

"Mistake?"

"There is nothing here!"

"Nothing there?"

"Nothing! See for yourself."

The old man stepped in, searched, and came out with drops of sweat upon his yellow forehead.

"Well?" exclaimed Capel, excitedly, as the old man stared in a dazed way.

"It is gone!" said the old lawyer, in a hoarse voice, and his hands trembling violently.

"Well, Mr Girtle," said Capel, at last, in a voice that he vainly strove to make firm; "what have you to say?"

"To say?" said the old lawyer, hastily.

"Oh, it is all a cock and bull story," cried Artis. "There never was any treasure."

"Silence, sir," cried the old lawyer recovering himself. "How can you speak like that in the presence of the dead?"

"Bah!" cried Artis. "Presence of the dead, indeed! Presence of a mummy. Would you have me pull a long face as I went through the British Museum?"

"I would have you behave — "

"You look here," cried Artis, sharply. "You are executor, and this treasure, if there was one, lay in your charge. It's nothing to me. If it were, I should call in the police."

"Mr Capel," cried the old lawyer excitedly, "I swear to you, sir, that the money and jewels were there a fortnight ago. I came down here with Ramo, and there lay the two cases with their contents."

"Well?" said Capel, "what then?"

"We carefully closed up the place."

"Then somebody must have been down since, and taken the treasure away."

"Only two men could have done this, sir, Ramo and myself."

"That throws it on to you," said Artis.

"And my reputation, sir, will bear me out when I proclaim my innocence."

"I don't know," said Artis. "Sudden temptation; kleptomania and that sort of thing."

The old lawyer turned his back.

"Mr Gerard Artis, this is no time for such re-marks as these," said Capel. "Mr Girtle, what have you to say?"

"At present, nothing, sir. I am astounded. You know we came down on that dreadful morning, and found the chamber intact; besides it could not have been forced."

"There were the keys," said Artis.

"But they have never left my person. There were but the two sets of keys — the Colonel's and mine. Those were the Colonel's set that we found upon Ramo."

"Rather strange that the Colonel should have given you a set," said Artis.

"No more strange than that a gentleman should trust a banker," said Capel.

"What, going to side with the lawyer?"

Capel made no reply, only gazed searchingly at the old executor.

"There may have been other keys, Mr Girtle."

"Oh, no. The place was made some years ago, for a sarcophagus, and the makers never imagined that it would be used for a safe."

There was a dead silence.

"Let us search again. The cases may have slipped aside."

"It is impossible," said the old lawyer; and as they two passed into the iron chamber, Artis exchanged a glance with Katrine, while the old butler stood looking dazed.

"You see," said Mr Girtle, holding down the light, "there is nowhere for the cases to have slipped; all is of plain, solid steel, without a corner or crack."

"But underneath," said Capel.

"Underneath? Look for yourself," said Mr Girtle; "where there is not solid steel there is solid iron, and beneath that, massive stone. The treasure seems to have been spirited away."

"That's it," said Artis. "The old man was not satisfied, and he got up out of his coffin and hid it somewhere else."

Capel caught Artis by the collar.

"I will not — " he began; but mastering his indignant anger he let fall his arm.

"There is nothing here," he said; "let us look about the outside."

That was the work of a minute, for on every hand there was the blank stone — wall, floor and roof, and the exterior of the iron safe or tomb was perfectly rectangular and smooth.

"What was the size of the cases?"

"One was about twelve inches by eight, and three or four deep, and the other rather smaller," replied the old lawyer; "both too large for me to have juggled them into my pockets when I opened the steel chest, Mr Artis."

"You held the keys, and if you meant to take the treasure, you had it before."

"Enough of this," cried Capel. "It is plain that the bequest has been taken away. Mr Girtle, we will finish at once — fulfill my uncle's commands. Come."

He went to the head of the oaken coffin, and

took one handle, when, influenced by his example, the others helped to raise it a little from the floor, and it was thrust in and onward, till it rested upon the bottom of the steel chest, nearly filling the space.

Capel stood on the right of the entrance, and for fully five minutes there was perfect silence in the solemn chamber.

"Go on, Mr Girtle," Capel said, at last, and the old man bent down, thrust the key in the end, gave a half turn, and the two ponderous sides slowly curved over till they were nearly together leaving only a few inches of the shining brass breastplate visible. Then there was a faint click, and the left side fell heavily, setting free the right, which descended with a loud clang, and closed tightly over a rebate in the lower side, so closely, that it was only by holding a candle near that the junction could be seen.

"Go on;" and the old lawyer again inserted a key.

There was no show of effort on his part, as the old lawyer turned the key, when the end of the iron chamber closed in tightly, and after once more examining the blank stone chamber, they slowly ascended the steps. Then the iron door was closed and locked, and Mr Girtle handed Capel the keys.

An hour later, a couple of masons were at work with the stones that were below in the locked-up cellar, and the next day they had filled in a wall of six feet thick, cemented over the face, so that only a dark patch showed where the entrance to the colonel's tomb had been.

# Chapter Thirteen.
# The Young Doctor.

"Look here," said Artis; "you mustn't be offended with me. I speak very plainly, and if I can be of any use to you, I will."

They were in the drawing-room, Preenham, having announced that the masons had left.

"I am not going to think of your remarks."

"I was thinking of going to-day," continued Artis; "but I feel now that I ought not to go and leave you in a regular hole like this."

"There is no need for you to stay."

"Well, no need, of course; but I suppose you will not kick me out."

"Of course not. You are welcome."

"That's right," said Artis. "You see," he continued, looking round to where Katrine and Lydia sat together, "I feel it due to myself to stop and show that I had no hand in that."

"No one accused you, Mr Artis."

"Oh, no, of course not; that would be too good a joke. Then I shall stay."

"Our case is different," said Lydia, turning red, and then pale. "Mr Capel, Miss D'Enghien and I, if we can be of no more use, would like to say good-bye this afternoon."

"But why?" cried Capel, as he glanced at the

speaker, and then fixed his eyes on Katrine. "There is no occasion for you to leave."

"I think Miss Lawrence is right," said Katrine.

"But I want help and counsel from both of you. You must not leave me yet."

"It is impossible for us to stay."

"Impossible! Why? Etiquette? Is not Mr Girtle here? Are not things as they have been since we met?"

"I did not know that Mr Girtle was going to stop?" said Katrine, softly. "If I felt that we could be of any service — "

"Then you will stay?" cried Capel, warmly.

Katrine hesitated, looked up, then down, raised, her eyes once more, and left her chair to take Lydia's hand.

"Let us go up-stairs," she said softly.

Lydia rose at once.

"You do not speak," said Capel.

Katrine did not answer till they reached the door, and then she raised her eyes to his with a long, timid look.

"If Lydia consents, so will I."

"And you will stay, Miss Lawrence, to help me?" cried Capel, warmly.

"I will," said Lydia, gravely.

"That's right," cried Capel, opening the door for them to pass out, and catching Katrine's eye for a moment as she passed.

"Curse her! She's playing a dangerous game," said Artis to himself, as he watched the ladies leave the room.

Glancing aside, he saw that the old lawyer was watching him narrowly.

"I suppose you are not glad that I am going to stay, Mr Girtle," he said.

"For some things I am," said the old man, coolly. "For others I am not."

Just then Capel returned.

The two girls separated as they reached their rooms, Katrine kissing Lydia's cheek, and then, as soon as she was alone, her countenance changed, and she sat gazing with glowing eyes, that seemed full of some purpose upon which she was bent.

At the same time Lydia Lawrence sat with her face buried in her hands, weeping silently and wishing that she were back in her country home.

Very little more was said below, for Mr Girtle had an engagement in the City, and left the young men together.

"You won't have a detective set to work?"

"No."

"Well, do as you like. I'm off for a run, to get rid of this gloom. Back to dinner."

"Thank goodness!" said Artis, breathing more freely, and five minutes after he was slowly crossing the square, wondering who the man was who had just gone up to the door he had left.

"I've seen his face before," he muttered. "Why, of course, the young doctor. What does he want?"

Capel was thinking of the fortune that had slipped through his fingers. Depressed, and yet at times overjoyed, for Katrine's glance had been full of hope. But he must trace the money that had been taken, and the gems — how lovely they would look on Katrine's neck!

He sighed as he pictured her thus adorned, and he was sinking into a day dream, when the door opened softly, and Preenham entered with the doctor's card.

"Doctor Heston? Show him up."

Capel motioned his visitor to a chair, when the keen-looking young doctor, who was watching him narrowly, said:

"I dare say you are surprised to see me here."

"Oh, no. A call?"

"I only make professional calls, Mr Capel, I have come to you on an important matter."

"Indeed!" exclaimed Capel.

"Yes. Respecting the death of one of those two men — the Indian, sir. I'm afraid there was some foul play there."

"Foul play? Why, he was killed with a life-preserver."

The doctor tapped with his fingers on his hat, as if he was beating a funeral march. Then, quickly:

"No, sir; the more I study this case, the more I feel convinced that he was not."

## Chapter Fourteen.
## A Clever Diplomatist.

"Doctor Heston, you surprise me. There was the inquest."

"Yes, where my opinion, sir, was overruled by the coroner and my colleague, both elderly medical men, sir, while I am young and comparatively inexperienced. You are disposed to think that this is a case of professional jealousy."

"I will be frank with you. I did think so."

"Exactly, but pray disabuse your mind. I am not jealous. I am angry with myself for giving way in that case. It seemed all very straightforward, but it was not."

"May I ask what you mean?"

"I mean, sir, that I am certain that our poor old Indian friend did not die from the blow that he received from that life-preserver."

"How then?" said Capel, huskily.

"It seems to me that he must have been poisoned in some way or another, and I could not rest without coming to you."

"Oh, impossible."

"Perhaps so, sir, but I am telling you what I believe. Do you think he had any enemies here?"

"Oh, no; the servants seemed to have been on friendly terms."

"Well, it hardly seems like it."

"That wretch must have yielded to a terrible temptation," said Capel, "and the other was defending his master's goods."

"What goods?" said the doctor.

Capel was silent.

"I see, sir, there is more mystery about this than you care to explain. Was there some heavy sum of money in the late Colonel's room, and were these two men in league?"

"I don't think they were in league."

"Was any one else interested in the matter?"

"Oh, no; impossible," said Capel, half aloud. "Dr Heston, I am afraid there is a good deal of imagination in what you say. Let me try and disabuse your mind."

"I should be glad if you could."

Capel paced the room for a few minutes.

"This has taken me quite by surprise, Doctor Heston," he said. "Give me a little time to think it over. Will you keep perfectly private all that you have said to me?"

"I don't like to suspect men unjustly, and yet I'm afraid I've done wrong, in giving him time," said the doctor, as he went down. "Well, a week is not an age."

As soon as he had left, Paul Capel let his head go down upon his hands, for his brain seemed to be in a whirl — the death of Ramo — the disappearance of the fortune — the visit of the doctor.

It only wanted this latter, with the hints he had thrown out, to fire a train of latent suspicion in the young man's mind.

There was that open window that the policeman had declared had not been used. Was he wrong? Had others been in the conspiracy and turned afterwards on Ramo and Charles? They might have been in the plot. Or, again, they might have been defending their master's wealth against the wretch who had escaped with the treasure by the open window.

Those three Italians!

Had they anything to do with the matter?

The old butler! He seemed so quiet and innocent! But often beneath an air of innocency, crime found a resting place.

Then he found himself suspecting Mr Girtle, and on the face of the evidence Capel laid before himself, the case looked very black. He knew everything; he held the keys — he, the old friend and companion, had been left merely a signet ring.

"Impossible!" cried Capel, half aloud; "I might as well suspect Artis, or Miss Lawrence, or Katrine herself."

"May I come in," said a voice that sent a thrill through the thinker, and Katrine D'Enghien stood in the doorway.

"Come in? Yes," cried Capel, advancing to meet her with open hands, and moved by an impulse that he could not withstand.

"Is anything the matter," she said simply.

"Yes — no — yes, a great deal is the matter," cried Capel. "There, I must speak to you."

"Mr Capel!" she said, half in alarm.

"Forgive me if I seem impetuous," he cried, "but I am greatly troubled in mind, and I feel as if I would give anything for the sympathy of one who would listen to my troubles, and help me with her counsel."

"Surely you have all our sympathy, Mr Capel," said Katrine, innocently.

"Yes, I hope so," he cried earnestly, "but I want more than that, Katrine. You must know that I love you."

"Mr Capel!"

"Pray do not be angry with me."

"Is this a time or season to make such a declaration to me, Mr Capel?" said Katrine, softly.

"For some things — no, for other things — yes. I am in such sore need of help and counsel, such as could be given me by the woman who returned my love. No, no; don't leave me. Hear me out. As soon as I heard that will read, it filled my heart with joy, for it told me that I was rich, and that these were riches which I could share with you. Then, when the discovery was made that the treasure had been stolen, it was not the wealth that I regretted, but I despaired because it seemed that you were farther from me. But listen to me. I am trying hard to discover how this large fortune has been swept away."

Katrine's eyes glittered.

"Help me in my endeavours, and tell me this — some day if I make the discovery, and am once more in a position to ask you to be my wife — you will listen to me?"

She raised her beautiful eyes to his, and he caught her hand.

It was withdrawn, and she said softly:

"I am sorry you should think me so sordid."

"Then you love me," he cried.

"I made no such confession. The man to whom I give my hand will not be chosen for the sake of his money."

"Then I may hope?" he cried.

"Mr Capel, is it not your duty to find your fortune?"

"Yes, but let me say, our fortune," he cried.

"Mr Capel, do not speak to me again like this. I should feel that I was standing in your light if I listened now."

"But at some future time?"

She looked at him softly, and his breath went and came fast, as her speaking eyes rested on his, and he saw the damask-red deepen in her cheeks.

"Wait till that future time comes," she whispered.

"And you will help me?" he cried.

"Yes," she said, at last, "I will help you — all I can."

He would have caught her in his arms, but she raised her hand.

"I thought we were to be friends."

"Friends," he whispered. "I love you."

"It must be then as a friend," she said, in her low voice; but there was that in her look which made Capel's heart throb, while, when she extended her hand, he kissed it, without being aware that Lydia had entered the room, and drawn back, with a weary look of misery in her face that she vainly sought to hide.

## Chapter Fifteen.
## In the Dark.

"Look here, Kate, I'm not going back till I've had a good try here to see if something can't be made out of this affair."

Katrine D'Enghien sat in the drawing-room of the Dark House, with her eyes half closed, as if listening to the ballad Lydia was singing in a low tone in the corner of the back room, while Capel stood by turning over the leaves.

The old lawyer was in another corner at a card-table, on whose green surface lay a heap of papers and parchments, one of which he took up from time to time, and laid down, after examining it by the light of the shaded lamp.

"You said only yesterday that you were sick of this domestic cemetery," said Katrine.

"So I am, for it's doleful enough for anything here, only it makes me mad to see such a wealth of art treasures and plate belonging to this fellow Capel."

"Then it is very evident that you did not filch the old man's treasure," said Katrine.

"Yes, my dear, very evident. If I had, I should not be here."

"Unless you thought it better for the sake of throwing people off the scent," said Katrine, with a peculiar look in his face.

"I say," he cried, returning the gaze, "what do

you mean? You don't think I killed those two fellows, and got the plunder, do you?"

"I don't know," she replied.

"Well, then, I didn't. I never had the chance."

"Or the brains to conceive such a *coup*."

"Look here," cried Artis.

"Don't speak so loud, Gerard."

"Oh, very well. But look here, Madam Clever, did you manage that bit of business?"

Katrine raised her soft, white hands.

"Don't do that," said the young man. "You make me want to kiss them."

"You would not be so foolish, now."

"I don't know. And look here, I don't like you being so thick with Capel."

"Don't you? He wants to marry me."

"I'll break his neck first."

"You will act sensibly and well, *mon cher*," said Katrine, "that is, if you mean that we are to be married by-and-by."

"Mean it? Of course."

"But not on a fortune of one hundred pounds each, *mon cher*."

"Good Heavens! No."

"Then hold your tongue, and say nothing."

"But I shall say something, if I see you working up a flirtation with that cad."

"You will say nothing, do nothing, see nothing. We cannot marry and starve."

"But tell me, Kate — honour bright — you don't care for this Capel?"

"I care for him!"

"Tell me, then, what do you mean to do?"

"Have my share of that money," said Katrine, with a peculiar hardening of her face.

"Bah! I don't believe the treasure ever existed. It was a craze on the old man's part."

"You must be careful. Don't say or do anything to annoy Paul Capel or Mr Girtle. We must stay here. It was no craze on the old man's part; maybe I can tell where the fortune is."

"What? You mean that?"

"Hush! I am working for us both."

"But tell me — "

"Hush! She has finished the song," said Katrine, leaning back and clapping her hands softly. "Thank you, thank you," she said. "Oh, what a while it is since I heard that dear old ballad."

The evening wore away till bed-time, when the butler brought in and lit the candles, according to his custom, Katrine and Lydia taking theirs, and going at once, and Gerard Artis following after partaking of a glass of soda-water, leaving the old lawyer and

Capel together.

They sat in silence for some minutes, when the old lawyer said:

"I do not seem to get any nearer to the unravelling of this knot, Mr Capel."

"Do you still adhere to the opinion that the treasure was there?"

"Yes; and we shall find it soon."

"By a masterly inactivity?"

"Oh, no," replied the old man, "for I am taking steps of my own to redeem myself. I don't think those jewels can be sold, or one of those notes changed, without word being brought to me."

Capel felt won by the old man's manner. He shook hands with him warmly, and said "Goodnight."

He went to the door with him, and saw the light shine on the thin, silvery hair as he went slowly up the staircase, while his candle cast a grotesque shadow on the wall. Then, as Capel listened, he heard the old man shut his chamber door, open it softly, and shut it again more loudly; while, with the great house seeming to be doubly steeped in darkness and silence, Paul Capel went back to the lounge in which he had been seated, leaving his chamber candle burning like a tiny star in the great sea of gloom, and sat back, thinking.

The candle burned lower as he thought on, ransacking his memory for some slight clue that would help him to find his lost fortune.

The candle went out.

Had he been asleep?

He could not say. He believed that he had been only thinking deeply. At all events, he was widely awake now, as he sat back listening to the heavy beating of his own heart, as he stared through the intense darkness towards the door, upon whose panel he had felt sure he had heard a soft pat, as if something had touched it.

A minute — it might have been half-an-hour, it seemed so long — and there was a faint rustling, and Paul Capel knew, as he stared through that intense darkness, that some one, or something, was coming silently towards where he sat.

# Chapter Sixteen.
## "You Here!"

Paul Capel was not superstitious, but a curious thrill ran through his nerves, and his first impulse was to leap up and shout, "Who's there?"

Then a thought flashed through his brain that whoever this was might have something to do with the disappearance of the treasure, and he told himself that he would wait, though the next moment he found himself frankly owning that a chill of dread had frozen his powers, and that he could not have moved to save his life.

A minute's reflection told him that it could not be a burglar. No one would come singly upon such a mission, and the marauder would have been provided with a dark lantern or matches. It must be some one in the house. The superstitious fancies were cleared away, as his heart gave a throb, with the hope that he might now find the clue to the mystery that was hanging over the place.

Thought after thought flashed through his brain, and, as they dazed him with the wild conjectures, the person, whoever it was, glided nearer and nearer, and all doubt fled, for, whoever it was, had stretched out a hand and touched the silver candlestick upon the table where he had set it down.

There was again silence, and then it seemed to Capel, as he sat there, that the nocturnal visitor had made the table a starting-point for a fresh departure in the dark, and was going from him toward the back drawing-room, in the left hand corner of which the old lawyer had sat that night.

Doubtless there are people who can weigh every act before they commit themselves to it, but the majority of us, even the most thoughtful, go on weighing a great many, and then in the most important moments of our lives forget all about the balance or the mental weights and scales, and so it was that, all in an instant, Paul Capel, unable longer to bear the mental strain, rose quickly from his seat, took two strides forward, and grasped at the intruder, exclaiming:

"Who's there?"

He touched nothing, he heard nothing, and the old chill came back for a moment or two with its superstitious suggestions; but he drew out a little silver match-box, which rattled as he opened it, shook a match into his moist hand, struck it, and the faint little star of light flashed out.

"Katrine, you here?" he exclaimed.

There were candles on an occasional table, and he lit one before the little wax match burned down, and then he remained speechless for the moment, gazing at Katrine D'Enghien, who stood within the back drawing-room, her long hair loosely knotted on her neck, her white arms outstretched before her, and half away from him. She stood motionless, as if turned to stone.

"Katrine!" he cried again.

He took a step or two towards her, his first impulse being to clasp her in his arms; but, as she stood motionless before him, draped in a long grey peignoir that swept the ground, there was something about her that repelled him, so that he stood staring at her unable to speak.

Suddenly she turned from him, and stood gazing at the corner where the piano stood, walked slowly towards it, and rested her hand upon it, remaining there motionless for a few moments till, catching up the candle, Capel went towards her, his pulses throbbing, and his temples seeming to flush as if a hot breath from a furnace had passed over them.

But before he reached her she turned slowly, and walked straight towards him, her eyes wide open, and gazing intently before her.

She would have walked right upon him, had he not given way, and then stood holding the candle, while she went deliberately to the fire-place, rested her hands upon the mantel-piece, and stood there holding one bare white foot towards the extinct fire as if to warm it.

Capel set down the candle and advanced towards her, when once more she turned and came straight towards him, and this time he took her in his arms and kissed her quickly and passionately upon her cheek and lips.

His arms dropped to his sides, though, for he felt that she was icily cold, and as involuntarily he gave place, and she walked slowly past him to the open door, out on to the broad landing, and as he caught up the candle and followed, he saw the tall grey figure go slowly on up and up the stairs, and when he followed it to the first landing it was on the one above, going slowly on to the bedroom at the end, through whose door it passed, and the lock gave a low, soft click.

Paul Capel went back into the drawing-room, feeling half stunned, and when he reached the middle of the room he paused, candle in hand, thinking.

"Asleep!" he said at last. "Asleep, and I dared to take her in my arms like that!"

Then, with an involuntary shiver, the young man turned quickly round, and went hastily up to his room, to lie till morning, tossing sleeplessly from side to side.

## Chapter Seventeen.
## The Tenth Night.

"It might be," thought Capel, as he dwelt upon the adventure of that night.

Katrine had descended to breakfast the next morning, and he fancied she blushed slightly as he pressed her hand; but she looked so frankly in his face that he could not but think that she was ignorant of what had taken place.

The days slipped by, and in company, by a private understanding, Capel and the old lawyer searched every article of furniture that could possibly have been made the receptacle of the lost treasure.

"I'll help you, of course, my dear sir," said the old man, "if you wish it; but I really think we shall do no good."

There had been several talks about breaking up the party, but Capel, as host, had always begged that his companions would stay, urging Mr Girtle to back him up by proposing that there should be no change until the whole of the business of the will was completed so far as the others were concerned.

"I shall find my share at last," Capel said, laughingly. "And besides, I have the house."

One afternoon, when Artis had accompanied the ladies for a drive, and the search was about to be recommenced, Mr Girtle sat down by his little table in the drawing-room and said:

"I have a little news for you, Mr Capel."

"What, have you found the clue?"

"Not yet," said the old man, quietly; "but I have found an angel."

"A what?"

"An angel. You did not know we had one in this house."

"Indeed, but I did," cried Capel.

"Ah, yes," said the old man, looking at him thoughtfully; "but I'm afraid we are not thinking of the same."

"Indeed, but we are," said Capel, warmly. "No one who has seen Miss D'Enghien — "

"Could hesitate to say that she is a very handsome woman," said the old lawyer, "but I was referring to Miss Lawrence."

"A lady for whom I entertain the most profound esteem," said Capel.

"Which will be strengthened, sir, when I tell you that she came to me and made a proposition that — "

The old lawyer's communication was checked by the announcement of a visitor for Mr Capel, and the doctor, Mr Heston, was ushered in.

His visit was not productive of much, for he had only to announce that he was more and more sure in his own mind that he was right, the result being that Capel asked him to wait before taking any further steps, and Dr Heston went away rather dissatisfied in his own mind.

"If he does not follow up my proposals," he said to himself, "I shall begin to think that he has some reason of his own for keeping the matter quiet."

The ladies returned directly the doctor had gone, and Artis, in pursuance of his instructions, made himself so agreeable to Capel that he did not leave him alone with the old lawyer, while at dinner and during the evening no opportunity was likely to occur for a private conversation.

"I'll see you directly after breakfast to-morrow morning, Mr Capel," the old man said. "I should prefer a quiet business chat with you, for the matter is important."

"I should like to have heard it at once," replied Capel, "but as you will."

Suspicion was very busy in the Dark House in those days, for the butler had found that for several nights past chamber candles had been burned down in the sockets in one of the candlesticks, which candlestick was left in the drawing-room, while a tall candlestick was afterwards taken up to the bedroom.

Preenham wanted to know why Mr Capel, "or the young master," as he termed him, should want to sit up so late, so he watched, and saw that, night after night, he stayed down in the drawing-room for hours. But he found out nothing, only that the cold struck, even through the mat, from the stone floor, and that he was chilly enough, when he went to bed in his pantry, to require a liqueur of brandy to keep off rheumatism and similar attacks.

For Capel had remained up after the others had gone, night after night; blaming himself for behaving in an unfair, unmanly spirit, but unable to control the impulse which led him to long for such another adventure as on that special night.

But after a long day, night watches grow wearisome to the most ardent lovers, and when, after nine nights spent in expectancy, there was no result — no soft, gliding step heard upon stair or floor, both Capel and Preenham grew weary, and retired to their couches like the rest.

It was on the tenth night that Capel, instead of going to bed at once, sat musing over the old lawyer's words.

Then he began thinking of the doctor's visit, and at last, taking out his watch, he saw it was close upon two.

The hour made him think of the night when he had encountered Katrine just at that time, and moved by some impulse, he knew not what, he went to his door, softly opened it, and gazed out on to the gloomy staircase, where all was silent as the grave.

No! There was the faint creak of a hinge that had been opened, and, with his heart seeming to stand still, Capel stood in the darkness listening, till, utterly wearied, he was about to close his door, when, so softly that he could hardly distinguish the sweep of the dress, something passed him, going straight to the stairs, and then he could just hear whoever it was descend.

## Chapter Eighteen.
## Nocturnal Proceedings.

There was not a sound to be heard as Paul Capel stole softly down in his dressing-gown, and, as he expected, the drawing-room door was closed, but not latched.

Pushing it softly, feeling certain that Katrine, if it was she, had entered there, he followed, and went on and on, till he was about in the middle of the room, and listening attentively.

He began to think that he must have been mistaken, when there was a faint rustle, and a heavy breath was drawn, the sounds coming from the lesser drawing-room.

He listened more intently, his heart beating heavily, and a strange singing in his ears.

Another sound as of something being touched.

The pen-tray on the little card-table where Mr Girtle sat and worked; and what was that?

Undoubtedly one of the keys that lay there. Another and another was touched, and as they were moved on the thin mahogany that formed the bottom of the receptacle for cards the sound seemed quite loud.

Then came a faint scraping sound, and he knew as well as if he had seen it, that a key was taken up.

Keys? Yes, there were several there which the old lawyer used. Capel recalled that the key of the plate closet had been placed there when Preenham had handed it over.

He listened, but there was no further sound. Yes; the low breathing could be heard, and it suddenly dawned upon Capel that Katrine had been approaching him — there she was close at hand. He had only to stretch forth his arms and the next instant she would have been folded to his breast.

It was a hard fight, but he had read of a sudden awakening under such conditions proving dangerous.

As he listened there was a faint rustling as the soft grey peignoir he knew so well passed over the thick carpet towards the door; and if the listener had any doubt, it was set aside by the light pat that he heard — it was a hand touching the panel.

Capel waited a minute, during which he heard the dress sweep against the edge of the door, and then the sound was quite hushed.

He knew what that meant, too; the door had been drawn to, and so he found it as he stepped lightly there, opened it, and passed out on to the great landing, where he strained his eyes upward to try and make out the graceful draped figure as it went up the winding staircase to the bedroom.

It was not so dark there, for a faint gloom — it could not be called light — fell from the great ground-glass sky-light, at the top of the winding staircase, like so much diluted darkness being poured down into a well.

That great winding staircase suddenly seemed

to him full of horror, as he stood there. It had never struck him before, but now, how terrible it seemed. That balustrade was so low. Suppose, poor girl, in her sleep, she should lean over it, and fall down onto the white stones, where the black fretwork of the glistening stove could be seen like a square patch against the white slabs.

There was no reason for such fancies, but Paul Capel's hands grew wet with a cold perspiration.

"I ought to have stopped her, and awakened her at any risk," he said, as he still gazed up the great staircase; and then his heart seemed to stand still, for there was a faint click, as of a lock shot back, and it came either from on a level with where he stood, or from down below.

In an instant he realised what had happened: Katrine had been to fetch the key of the late Colonel's chamber, and had gone in there.

He hesitated a moment, and then, going close, he softly touched the door, and felt it yield.

Just then there came a faint scratching noise, and there was a gleam of light, showing him that the heavy curtain was drawn.

Then the light shone more clearly, and pressing the door a little more open, he glided through.

He was about to peer out softly, when the light was set down, he heard the soft rustle of the dress, an arm was thrust round from the far side of the curtain, and the door was carefully closed.

"The work of a spy," he said. But a slight sound

attracted his attention, and his curiosity mastered all other feelings.

Gently sliding his hand into his pocket, he drew out a penknife, and cut gently downwards, making a slit a few inches in length.

This he drew slightly apart and gazed through, to see that Katrine was standing with her back to him, in the act of opening one of the large cabinets at the side of the bed.

# Chapter Nineteen.
## Birds of Prey.

Travellers in Mayfair will have noticed that every here and there old-fashioned, snug looking hostelries exist in out-of-the-way places — at the corner of a mews, in a private street, where they do not seem to belong; and they are generally kept by ex-butlers, who have taken wives, joined their savings, and gone into business with the brewers' help.

In the parlour of the "Four-in-Hand," Lower Maybush street, a party of gentlemen's servants were playing bagatelle upon a bad board in a very smoky atmosphere, while a knot of three men sat at one of the old, narrow, battered mahogany tables in a corner, drinking cold gin and water, and smoking bad cigars.

One was a little sharp-eyed, round-headed man, smartly dressed, and evidently rather proud of a large gilt pin in his figured silk tie. Another was tall and not ill-looking; he might have been a valet, for there was a certain imitation gentility about his cut — a valet whose master had been rather addicted to the turf, and this had been reflected on his man to the extent of trousers rather too tight, short hair, and a horseshoe pin with pearl nails. The third was rather a shabby-looking man of forty, undoubtedly a gentleman's servant out of place, carrying the sign in the front of the reason why, in the shape of a nose unduly ripened by being bathed in glasses of alcoholic drink.

"Knew him how long, did you say?" said the

tall man, tapping his chin with an ivory-handled rattan-cane.

"Ten years, poor chap," said the ex-servant. "It was very horrid."

"Here, never mind that," said the brisk little man. "We don't want horrors. Touch the bell, Dick. Come, old fellow, sip up your lotion, and we'll have them filled again. That cigar don't draw. Try one of these. Here! three fours of gin cold," he cried to the landlord, and as soon as the glasses were refilled, and cigars lighted, the conversation went on, to the accompaniment of rattling balls and laughter from the bagatelle players.

"Well," said the tall man, in a low voice, "you can do as you like, my lad, but I should have thought that, hard up as you are, and I should say without much chance of getting another crib — say at present — you'd have been glad to earn a honest quid or two."

The shabby-looking man shook his head.

"Here, you're always putting on the pace too much, Dick," said the little man. "A fellow wants a little time. He's on, you see if he isn't. My respects to you, Mr Barnes. Hah! nice flavoured drop of gin that."

"You see, you know the house well," continued the tall man. "Often been, of course?"

"Oh, yes; had many a glass of wine there, when poor Charles was alive."

"Rather a bit of mystery, that," said the little

man. "I put that and that together, and I set it down that he was trying the job on his own account, and muffed it."

The shabby man shuddered, and took a hearty draught of his gin and water.

"There would be only us three in the game," said the tall man softly, "and it would be share and share alike. Why, if we worked it right, it would set you up. Might take a pub on it."

"Eh?" said the shabby man.

"I say you might take a pub — and drink yourself to death," was added aside.

The little man winked at his tall companion, unobserved by the other, who looked dreamy.

"Bars at all the lower windows, eh?"

"Yes, yes. You couldn't get in there," was the quick reply.

"More ways of killing a cat than by hanging it. Look here, my lads, there's a stable to let in the mews at the back."

The shabby man looked up quickly.

"I had a look at it to-day. Any one could easily get to that window looking on the leads."

"But that's the window where — "

"Well, dead men tell no tales, and they don't get in the way. That's the place."

"Oh, no," said the shabby man.

"Bah! you're not afraid. I tell you it would be as easy as easy. You can give me a plan of the place, and all about it, and — why, it's child's play, my lad, and won't hurt anybody. Take everything out of that stable, and have a cart in the coach-house. I say — touch that bell again, old man — you are not going to let a fortune slip through your fingers, I know."

The three occupants of the corner soon after rose to go, halting half-way down the street, where the tall man said: —

"There's half a sovereign to keep the cold out till then. Twelve o'clock, mind, punctual."

The shabby man slouched away, while the little fellow rubbed his hands.

"There's half a ton of it there," he whispered.

"Think he'll stand to it?"

"No fear, now we've got him over his fright. By jingo, I'm only afraid of one thing."

"What's that?"

"That some one else will be on the job."

## Chapter Twenty.
## Asleep or Awake?

It was a painful, and, Paul Capel thought, a degrading position; but he blamed his passion, telling himself that it was his duty to watch her, in this sleep-walking state, lest ill should befall.

How thoroughly awake she seemed to be. Her every act was that of a person perfectly herself, and eager to find something that was hidden.

Softly and quickly she examined the cabinet, opening drawer after drawer, and taking out one after the other, to see whether there was a concealed cavity behind.

Next she knelt down before a large carved oak chest, and Capel saw how carefully she searched that, and examined top and bottom to see whether either was false.

This done, she walked to the bed, and stood pondering there. Crossing to the built-up portal, she drew the curtain aside, revealing the half-dry cement.

She shook her head, and walked to the window, where she carefully rearranged the heavy folds there, to keep the rays of light from passing out and betraying her task to any one who might be at the upper windows of some house. The act displayed the working of a brain that, if slumbering, still held a peculiar activity of an abnormal kind.

Once or twice he caught sight of Katrine's eyes, that were not as he had seen them on that other night, wide open, and staring straight before her, but bright, eager, and full of animation.

"She must be awake," he thought; and the idea was strengthened as he saw her throw herself down upon a chair, and with a peculiar action of her hands indicative of disappointment, rest her elbows on her knee, her chin upon her clenched fists, and there she bent down, her face intent, her brows knit, and looking ten years older, as the candle cast a curious shadow on her countenance.

Then the lover intervened on her behalf.

No; she could not be. To suppose that she was awake was to credit her with being deceitful — with cheating him into the belief that night that she was asleep.

He was about to spring out, throw himself at her feet, and waken her with his caresses, but a chilling feeling of repulsion stayed him. It might work mischief in the terrible fright it would give her at being awakened in that gloomy room. And besides, what a place to select for his passionate avowals. It was secret and silent, the very home for such a love as his; but there was the terrible past.

Where she was seated, but a short time back, there lay the ghastly body of the murdered man. Behind her was the bed where so recently a strange occupant was stretched, and beneath it lay that other lately discovered horror. Beyond that built-up wall was the Colonel's tomb.

Love was impossible in such a place as that; and did he want confirmation of the fact that Katrine was a somnambulist, he felt that he had it here before him. For no girl of her years would dare to come down in the dead of the night, and enter that room, haunted as it was with such terrible memories.

He stood watching her as she crouched there, looking straight before her, and as she suddenly sprang up, and went to a picture painted upon a panel in the wall, he found himself growing excited by the fancy that, perhaps, in the clairvoyant state of sleep, she might be able to discover the mystery that had baffled them all.

He stood there wrapt in his thoughts, till he saw her turn from the frame, that she had tried to move in a dozen different ways, her fingers playing here and there with marvellous quickness about the corners and prominent bits of carving, as if she expected that any one might prove to be a secret spring.

Again she tried another picture; darted to the group of statuary in the corner, and tried to lift it back, as if expecting that which she sought might be hidden beneath it; and again there was the movement, full of dejection and despair, as she stood facing him with the light full upon her eyes.

She turned away, despondently; and then started upright, with her eyes flashing, and one hand raised in the involuntary movement of one who listens intently to some sound.

Had she heard something, or was it fancy — a part of her dream?

Paul Capel thought the latter, for, light as a

fawn, he saw Katrine dart across the room to where the candle stood.

The next moment they were in total darkness.

## Chapter Twenty One.
## What the Sound was.

A faint rustle was plainly heard, as Capel drew aside the curtain. Then the sound ceased, but he felt that as he had taken a step to the left, Katrine must be exactly opposite to him. In another moment she would come forward and touch him, for he could not move from his position. If he stood aside she would pass him and fasten him in the room.

He listened in the intense darkness, and could just detect the short, hurried breathing of one who was excited by dread.

But as he listened in the darkness, clear now of the heavy curtain, he heard another sound — a peculiar scraping sound, that seemed to come from outside the window.

It was that which had alarmed Katrine, and made her extinguish the light.

The noise ceased. Then it was repeated, and directly after, sounding muffled by the heavy curtain, the window rattled a little in its frame, as if shaken or pressed upon by some one outside.

The panting grew louder, there was a warm breath upon Capel's cheek, and the next moment he held Katrine in his arms.

She uttered a low cry of fear, and struggled to escape.

"Hush!" he whispered. "You have nothing to fear. Are you awake?"

There was no answer; only a vigorous thrust from the hands placed upon his chest, and he felt that she was trying to open the door, trembling violently the while.

"Katrine," he whispered, "why do you not trust me? Wake up. There is nothing to fear."

He tried to clasp her in his arms again, but with a quick movement she eluded him, and as he caught at her again, it seemed as if the great curtain had been thrust into his arms, for he grasped that, and as he flung it away, the door struck him in the face, and then closed, he heard it locked, and the key withdrawn.

Then he stood listening, for the window rattled again, and he wondered that the noise he had made in his slight struggle with Katrine had not been heard by whoever was on the sill.

There was a bell somewhere in the room; but if he rang, and roused up the butler, the man would be horrified at hearing his old master's bedroom bell ringing in the dead of the night.

Even if that had not been the case, what excuse could he make? And could he explain his position to Mr Girtle without making him the confidant of all that had passed? And how could he relate to any one that Katrine had been wandering about the house in the middle of the night? What would Mr Girtle say? Would he think it was somnambulism?

No; he could not ring. It was impossible; and all the while there was that strange noise outside, muffled by the curtain.

He walked cautiously through the intense darkness towards the window, till he could touch the curtain, and then, passing to the left, he softly drew it a little inward, and looked out.

It was almost as dark out there as in; but there was a faint glow from the lamps beyond the tall houses that closed in the back, and against this he could dimly see the figure of a man, standing on the sill, while, more indistinctly and quite low down, there were the heads and shoulders of two more.

It seemed to him that the man standing on the sill was trying to pass some instrument through between the two sashes, so as to force back the window-catch.

What should he do?

Give the alarm down-stairs he could not, without compromising Katrine.

Alarm the nocturnal visitors?

That would be to give up a chance of getting hold of the clue.

What should he do?

Be a coward, or, now that the opportunity had come, make a bold effort to capture these intruders?

Three to one. Yes; but he was in the fort, and they had to attack, and could he secure one, bribery or punishment would make him tell all.

There was the sound going on at the window, which was resisting the efforts, and, with palpitating heart and heavy breathing, Capel asked himself the questions again. Should he be cowardly, or brave, and make a daring effort to gain that which was his, from the information these people could give?

There was a grating and clicking still going on as he stepped cautiously across the room, the sound guiding him to the stand where his uncle's old East India uniform and accoutrements were grouped, and the next minute his hands rested upon a pistol.

Useless, for it was old-fashioned and uncharged.

That was better! His hand touched the ivory hilt of the curved sabre.

For a time the blade refused to leave its sheath; then it gave way a little, and he drew it forth, laid the scabbard on the floor, passed his hand through the wrist-knot, and thought that he would have to strike hard, for a cavalry sabre is generally round-edged and blunt.

As he thought of this, he touched the edge of the sword with his thumb, to find that this was no regulation blade, but a keen-edged tulwar, set in an English hilt, and, armed with this, Paul Capel felt himself fully a match for those who were working away at the window, which did not yield.

*Creak — Crack — Crack!*

The catch flew back, and there was a pause, during which Capel drew near with the blade thrown over his left shoulder, ready for delivering the first cut at the man who entered.

Then the window glided up, the great curtain

was drawn by an arm in his direction, partly cover-
ing him, and a light flashed across the room.

## Chapter Twenty Two.
## A Blank Adventure.

The light played on the blade of the keen-edged sword, as if it were phosphorescent, but the lambent quivering was not seen by the holder of the lantern, who hid Capel with his own hand as the light was flashed upon the bed and into the corners of the room, and then turned off.

"All right, boys," was whispered, and a man swung himself into the room. "Be quick, and shut the window."

A second man crept softly in, and the third was half in, when he slipped, threw out his hand to save himself, struck against one of his companions and drove him back against the curtain and upon Capel.

"Light! Barkers! Some one here."

Capel heard the words, saw the flash, and struck at the hand that held it.

The blade fell heavily upon the lantern and dashed it to the floor, where it went out.

Raising the sword he struck again, but as he did so, one of the men sprang at him, and the blow that fell was upon the fellow's shoulder, and with the hilt of the sword.

Capel was borne back by the man's fierce spring, his feet became entangled in the curtain and he fell heavily, with his adversary upon him.

"Quick, Morris," whispered a voice.

"No, no. Curse you. Shut the window. There's only one. Where's your matches? Quick, light the glim! Ah, would you? Lie still and bite that. You just move again and I'll pull the trigger."

The barrel of a revolver had been thrust between Capel's teeth, and as he lay back with the man on his chest, half stunned, helpless and despairing, he saw indistinctly the figure against the window, heard the sash slide down, and the darkness was complete as the curtain was drawn over the panes. Then there was the faint streak of light as a match was struck, the bull's-eye lantern was picked up and re-lit, and the bright rays once more played all about the room.

The man who held it then went to the door and listened.

"It's all right," he whispered. "You said nobody can't hear what goes on in this room. These curtains would suffocate a trumpet. Here, you," he cried to the third man, "don't stand shivering like that. Take that carving-knife out of his hand. Pull the trigger, Dick, if he stirs."

This to the man kneeling on Capel's chest.

Capel lay absolutely powerless at that moment; but, as the third fellow caught him by the wrist, the young man wrenched his head on one side, and heaved himself up, so that he partially dislodged the ruffian who held him down. At the same time he swung the sabre round, driving the third back, and striking the principal adversary so sharp a blow that he slipped aside, and Capel leaped to his feet.

At that moment the light was turned off, and there was a rush made to get beyond his reach.

Capel also took advantage of the total darkness to step back, but he held the weapon ready for a cut, should an attack be made.

As he stood there, panting, a low whisper rose from the direction of the door, and he just caught its import, "Give me the light."

There was a click directly after, and then from about the middle of the room the dazzling light of the bull's-eye shone out full upon Capel as he stood with upraised sword, while his assailants were in the dark.

"Now, then," said the voice which he recognised as that of the man who had held the pistol to his mouth, "throw down that tool."

"Give up, you scoundrel!" cried Capel. "You can't escape."

"Can't we?" said the man, between his teeth, "More can't you. Now, then, will you throw down that sword?"

"No," said Capel, furiously. "You've walked into a trap, so give up."

"Go on," said the voice of the lesser man.

At that moment there was a bright flash of light, a sharp report, and Capel felt a sensation as if he had been struck a violent blow on the left shoulder, which half spun him round, while the round, glistening disc of light seemed to have darted back to the side of the bed.

Half stunned, but full of fight, Capel turned and made for the light once more, when there was another flash, a quick shot, and this time the blow seemed to have fallen on the top of his head, and, stunned and helpless, the sword dropped from his hand, and he fell on a chair, and from that on to the floor.

"You've killed him! You've killed him!"

"Good job, too. Think I wanted my skin turned into pork crackling with that sword? Hold yer row, will yer, or — "

"We shall be taken and hung. Oh, my arm!"

"Look here, my dear pal," said the little man; "if you want to preach, just wait till this job's done. Throw the light on the door, Dick."

"I dunno which is doors and which is windows, with all these curtains. Oh, that's it, is it? Quiet, will you?"

He stood listening attentively. "It's all right. There isn't a sound."

"Let's go then, at once."

"What, empty? Not me, eh, Dick?"

"'Taint likely. Wait till I've got two more cartridges in. That's it — Now then, business."

"But this poor fellow?"

"He's not killed, only quieted. Now, then, what is there here?"

They made a hurried search of the room, but with the exception of the silver tops of the bottles of the Colonel's dressing-case, there was nothing to excite their cupidity. Then Capel's pockets were searched, but watch and purse were in his chamber, while, though the Colonel's room was full of costly objects, they were not of the portable nature that would have made them valuable to the men.

"Now then," said the tall man, quickly, "it's of no use; we must go down. Where are the keys?"

The little man took a bunch from the bag.

"But, suppose the old man's awake?" whispered the shivering ex-servant, faint from his wound.

"Well, if he is, we must persuade him to go to sleep, somehow, till we've done. Here, you come and hold the light while I hand him the keys."

The trembling man took the lantern, while his leader went down on one knee; and as his little companion handed him false keys and picklocks, he busied himself trying to open the door.

"Keep that light still, will you?" he cried menacingly. "Why, you're making it dance all over the door. I want it on the key-hole, don't I?"

Then the light shone full on the lock for a minute or two, not more, for he who held it kept turning his head to see if Capel was moving.

This brought forth a torrent of whispered oaths from both men.

"Here, let me have a try," whispered the little man. "I can open it if you'll hold this blessed glim still. I never see such a cur."

Then, in the coolest manner possible, he took the other's place, and tried key after key, picklock after picklock, and ended by throwing all into the bag with a growl of disgust.

"It's one of them stoopid patents," he cried. "Here, give us a james."

A strong steel crowbar in two pieces was screwed together, and its sharp edge inserted between the door and the post, but the great, solid mahogany door stood firm, only emitting now and then a loud crack, sharp as that given by a cart whip, as the men strained at it in turn.

"Here, let's try a saw. Centre-bit!"

A centre-bit was fitted into a stock, and a hole cut right through. Into this, after much greasing, a key-hole saw was thrust, and, not without emitting a loud noise, the work of cutting began, the sawdust falling lightly on the lion's skin; but at the end of a few seconds a dull, harsh sound told that the saw was meeting metal, and a fresh start had to be made.

For fully two hours did the men work to get through, boring and sawing in place after place, but always to find that the door was strengthened in all directions with metal plates; and at last the task was given up. "Look here," growled the leader of the party, "that bed isn't used. I want to know how that chap got in. He hasn't any key."

"Can't you get the door open, then?" said the third man, after the other had shaken his head.

"Why, don't you see we can't?"

"But we shall get nothing for our trouble."

"Nothing at all," said the tall man, quietly.

"But — "

"There, that'll do. First of all, you were so precious anxious to go. Now you know we can't get down, you're all for the job. I say, is this the room where the murder was?"

"Yes; don't talk about it."

"Why not? We haven't done another. He'll come round."

"What next, Dick?"

"Cut," was the laconic reply.

"When there's all that plate asking of us to make up a small parcel and carry it away?"

"Don't patter. Got all the tools?"

"Yes."

"Then come along."

The light was played upon Capel's insensible face for a few moments, and then, to the intense relief of the ex-servant, the lantern was placed in the bag with the burglars' tools, and the window being thrown open, one by one stole out, the last closing the window behind him, leaving Capel lying helpless and insensible in the locked-up room.

## Chapter Twenty Three.
## Waiting for Breakfast.

"Such a bright cheery morning, Lydia," said Katrine, knocking at the bedroom door. "Oh, you are up. Breakfast must be ready."

The two girls descended, to find that they were first.

"Nobody down," cried Katrine, "and I am so hungry. Oh, how wicked it seems on a morning like this to keep out all the light and sunshine."

Just then, old Mr Girtle came in, looking, as usual, very quiet and thoughtful; and after a while Artis came down, looking dull and sleepy.

"Where's the boss?" he said, suddenly.

"The what? — I do not understand you," said the old lawyer.

"The master — the guardian of this tomb. Where's Capel?"

"Oh," said the old lawyer. "Possibly the fine morning may have tempted him to take a walk."

"Are we going to wait for Capel?" said Artis.

"I'm so hungry, I feel quite ashamed," said Katrine; "but I think we ought to wait."

"There is nothing to be ashamed of in a healthy young appetite, my dear young lady," said the old lawyer. "I have been reading in my room since six, and I should like to begin. I don't suppose he will be long. Mr Capel out, Preenham?"

"I think not, sir," said the butler, who was bringing in a covered dish.

"Perhaps you had better tell him that we are all assembled. He may have overslept himself."

At the end of five minutes the old butler was back to say that Mr Capel had not answered when he knocked.

"He may be ill," said Lydia anxiously, and then, catching Katrine's eye, she coloured warmly.

Preenham gave Artis a meaning look, and that gentleman followed him out.

"What is it?"

"Mr Capel hasn't been to bed all night, sir."

"Not been to bed all night, Preenham?" said the old lawyer, who had followed. "Did you let him out last night?"

"No, sir."

"Then how can he have gone out? I saw that the door was fastened after you had gone to bed, and it was still fastened when I came down at six."

"And at seven too, sir," said the butler.

"He must be in the house," said Artis. "Go and look round."

"Is Mr Capel ill?" said Katrine.

"No, no, my dear, I think not," said the old lawyer. "I'll go, too, and see."

"It is very strange," said Katrine, turning to

Lydia, who looked ashy pale. "I hope nothing is the matter, dear."

She seemed so calm that Lydia took courage and returned to the breakfast-table, while, followed by the old lawyer and Preenham, Artis examined the dining-room and study, then ascended to the first floor, tried the Colonel's door, found it fast, and went on into the drawing-room.

"I tried that door," he said grimly, "because that is the chamber of horrors."

"It is locked, and the key is in my table," said the old lawyer, and then they searched the other rooms, finding Capel's watch, purse and pocket-book, and looked at each other blankly.

"He must be out," said Artis.

"No, sir; here's his hat and stick."

Artis stopped, thinking, and then bounded up the stairs again to the Colonel's door.

"I thought so," he said. "There's something wrong here. Look." He pointed to several holes through the mahogany door, the mark of a saw scoring the panels, and the reddish dust on the lion-skin mat. "Is any one here?" he cried, knocking. "I say! Is any one here? Pah! Look at that!"

He uttered a cry, almost like a woman, as he pointed to a place where the lion-skin rug did not reach, and there, dimly seen by the gloomy light thrown by the stained-glass window, was a little thread of blood that had run beneath the door.

## Chapter Twenty Four.
## Doctor and Nurse.

The old lawyer ran from the door with an alacrity not to be expected in one of his years, and returned directly with the key that he had found in his table.

"Give it to me," said Artis huskily, and snatching the key he tried to insert it, but his hand trembled so that he did not succeed, and the next moment he shrank away.

"Here, open that door, Preenham," he said.

"I daren't, sir, I daren't indeed. Ah, poor young man!"

"Give me the key," said the old lawyer firmly, and taking it, he tried the door, to find that the lock had been tampered with, so that it was some minutes before he could get it to move.

"Hadn't I better fetch the police, sir?" faltered the butler.

"No; stop," said the old lawyer, turning the handle. "There is some one against the door."

He pushed hard, and with some effort got it open so that he could have squeezed in.

"It is all dark," he said. "No it is the curtain," and forcing his way through, he drew back the hangings from the window.

"It's poor Capel — dead!" whispered Artis, who had followed. "Here, Preenham, come in," he cried angrily. "Oh, how horrible — poor lad!"

The lawyer saw the naked sword lying on the carpet; that the drawers and cabinet had been ransacked; and that the window was not quite shut down.

He took this in at a glance as he ran to where Capel lay close to the door, where he had dragged himself sometime during the early hours of the morn, to lie exhausted after vainly trying to raise the alarm.

"He's dead, sir, dead!" groaned the butler.

"Hush!" cried the old lawyer harshly. "He's not dead. Mr Artis, you are young and active. Quick. That doctor, Mr Heston. You know where he lives. You, Preenham, brandy. Stop. Tell the ladies Mr Capel is ill. Nothing more. Don't spread the alarm."

"Is anything very serious the matter?" said a voice at the door.

"Yes — no, my dear. Go away now," cried the old lawyer, "Mr Capel is ill."

"There is something terribly wrong again," said a deeper voice, and, white as ashes and closely followed by Katrine, Lydia came in.

She uttered a faint cry, and then wrested herself from Artis, who tried to stop her.

"No," she cried, imperiously, changed as it were in an instant from a shivering girl into a thoughtful woman. "Quick: go for help. Mr Girtle, what can I do?"

"Yes, let me help too," said Katrine. "What is it; has he tried to kill himself?"

"No," cried Lydia, turning upon her fiercely. "He was too true a man."

"I'm afraid there has been an attempt made by burglars," said the old lawyer, "and that our young friend has been trying to defend the place; but — but he was locked in here — the key was in my table — and — and — I'm afraid I'm growing very old — things seem so much confused now."

He put his hand to his head for a few moments and looked helplessly from one to the other. Then his customary *sang froid* seemed to have returned.

"This is not a sight for you, ladies," he said. "Pray go back."

"I am not afraid, Mr Girtle," said Katrine, with a slight shudder as she looked eagerly about the room.

For her answer, Lydia took water from the wash-stand, and began to bathe the blood-smeared face, kneeling down by Capel's side.

Just then Preenham entered with decanter and glass, the former clattering against the latter, as he poured out some of the contents.

Holding a little of the brandy to Capel's clenched teeth, Mr Girtle managed to trickle through a few drops at a time, while Lydia continued the bathing, and Katrine stood, like some beautiful statue, gazing down at them with wrinkled brow and clasped hands.

By this time, the knowledge that something was wrong had reached the women-servants, and they had both come to the door.

"No, no; keep them away, Preenham," said Mr Girtle, in answer to offers of assistance. "You go down, too, and be at the door, ready to let the doctor in."

"Yes, sir, I will," said the old butler, piteously; "but my young master — will he live?"

"Please God!" said the lawyer simply.

"But he is not dead, sir?"

"There is your answer, man," said Mr Girtle, for just then Capel uttered a low moan.

The old butler bent down on one knee, and Lydia darted at him a grateful look, as she saw him lift and press one cold hand, and then, laying it down, he rose, and went out of the room on tiptoe, raising his hands and his face towards Heaven.

"Was he stabbed — with that sword?" said Lydia, in a hoarse whisper.

"No, I think not. The doctor must soon be here," was the reply.

In fact, five minutes later there was a quick knock at the door, and Dr Heston hurried in, followed by Artis.

"Give me the room," he said quickly. "Ladies, please go."

Katrine turned slowly, and glanced at Lydia.

"I may stay, Doctor Heston," she said. "I may be of use."

"No words now," he said, sharply. "By-and-by you will be invaluable. Well there, stay."

He had thrown off his coat and rolled up his sleeves as he spoke, and as Lydia bent her head and stood waiting, Katrine left the room. Then the deft-handed medico was busy with his examination.

"Head literally scored with a bullet," he said.

"Not a cut?" whispered Mr Girtle, pointing to the sword.

"Bless me, no. Scored by a bullet. An inch lower — hallo! What have we here?"

He took out a knife and cut through the clothes, where he could not draw them away from where the blood had oozed out just below the left shoulder.

"Hah! Yes! Bullet. Entered here; passed out. No! Here it is. Just below the skin."

He had raised the sufferer, and found that the bullet had passed nearly through, and was visible so near the surface that a slight cut would have given it exit.

"Nothing vital touched, I think," said the doctor, busying himself about the wound in the shoulder.

"Ah! That's right, madam. Nothing like a woman's hand, after all, about a sick man. Why, this must have happened hours ago."

The doctor chatted away, quickly, but his hands kept time with his voice. He had laid down a small case of instruments with a roll of linen, and turning from the arm once more, he rapidly clipped away the hair, and dressed the wound in the head, a wound so horrible that Artis shuddered, turned to the brandy decanter that the old butler stood holding with a helpless, dazed look, and poured out a good dram, while Lydia knelt there, very pale, but calmly holding scissors, lint or strapping, to hand as they were required.

"Now for the bullet," said the doctor in a cheerful, airy way. "Mr Artis, just lend a hand here. Or, no; you look upset. Put down that decanter, butler! This isn't a dinner-party. That's right. Now kneel down here."

He softly raised Capel, and placed him in a convenient position before turning to Lydia.

"Really, I think you would prefer to go now?"

The girl's lips seemed to tighten and she shook her head.

"As you please;" said the doctor testily. "I have no time to waste. A little back, Mr Girtle; I want all the light I can have. Yes, that's plain enough," he muttered, as with one hand resting on the injured man's shoulder where the bullet made quite a little lump, he stretched out the other, and from where it nestled in the case, fitted amongst so much purple velvet, he took out a small knife.

There was a pleasant look of satisfaction in the doctor's face, as he took out the knife, but the next moment he turned with an angry flash upon Lydia.

It was the natural instinctive act of one who loves seeking to protect the object loved. For as Dr Heston took the knife in his hand, Lydia's eyes dilated, and she leaned forward, caught the doctor's arm, and gazed at the keen little blade with dilated eyes.

"My dear young lady, are you mad?" cried the doctor, testily.

She raised her eyes to his in a look so full of appeal, that he could read it as easily as if she had given it with the interpretation of words.

He was not accustomed to argue in a case like this, but the girl's loving attempt to protect the insensible man, touched him to the heart; and dropping his sharp, imperious manner, he said gently:

"But, don't you see? It is to do him good."

Lydia's hand trembled, but she still grasped the doctor's arm.

"Come, come," he said, smiling. "You must not be alarmed. Do you want the bullet to stay in and irritate the whole length of the wound?"

She gave her head a sharp shake.

"Well, then, be sensible, my dear girl. There, get me a bit of lint," he continued, "and you shall see how easily and well I will do this. That's better. Why, taking a tooth out is ten times worse. This is a mere trifle. There, that's a brave little woman. He will not even feel it."

Lydia's hand had dropped from the doctor's arm, and she drew a long breath, watching him as if her eyes were drawn to his knife, while he bent over Capel.

In a few minutes more the patient was lifted upon the bed, and Lydia stood there with her hands clasped in dread, for it seemed ominous to her that Capel should be compelled to lie there.

"Can he not be taken up to his room?"

"No, my brave little nurse, no. It would have been extremely nice for him, but what he requires now is absolute rest and quiet. Come, come. You are too strong-minded a little woman to be superstitious. Go where you will, in old houses, there has generally been a death in some of the bedrooms; but believe me, that does not affect the living. Why, if that were the case, what should we do at the hospitals? You are going to install yourself here, then, as nurse? That's right. Let my instructions be carried out, and I'll come in again at noon."

Whispered conversation went on all through the house that day, but though there had been the attempt at burglary, Mr Girtle hesitated about calling in the police again, and on consulting the doctor, he quite agreed that it would be better not to have them there.

"It will only disturb my patient," he said, "and, depend upon it, with a light and people sitting up, the scoundrels will not come again."

"Well," said Mr Girtle, "we will not communicate with the police at present."

The doctor came in at one, and again at five; and, on leaving, looked rather serious.

"If he is not different to this at about nine, when I come in again, I'll get Sir Ronald Mackenzie to see him. I'll warn him at once that he may be wanted."

"Then you think his case serious?"

"Brain injuries always are."

At nine o'clock, when the doctor came, his manner startled Lydia, who had patiently watched the sufferer all day.

"Yes," he said; "I will have Sir Ronald's opinion. I shall be back in half-an-hour."

He left the room and hurried down-stairs, while Lydia bent down and laid her cheek against the patient's burning hand. He was delirious now, and talking loudly and rapidly.

"Yes, it is there," he kept on saying. "Count four stones from the left, press on the fifth, and it will swing around. I have it safely — do you hear? — safely."

This went on over and over again, and as Lydia listened, something, she knew not what, made her turn her head, when it seemed to her that one of the bed curtains trembled, and that, in the gloom, a hand was softly drawing one back, that the sick man's words might be more plainly heard.

## Chapter Twenty Five.
## High Words.

Looking again in the direction of the hand, but telling herself that it was fancy, Lydia sat down to wait anxiously for the doctor's return, while Capel went on, talking more or less incoherently.

"You know I love you," he said softly. "Katrine — darling — you will be my wife. Let the world go its own way, what is it to us?"

Lydia's head sank lower, as the tears of misery began to fall fast.

"The treasure," he cried, suddenly. "Ha — ha — ha! Let them search for it — months — years. They will never find it. I have it safely. Here. I'll tell you."

He beckoned with his finger as he talked on, rapidly; and as Lydia raised her saddened countenance, she saw that he was gazing at vacancy and gesticulating with his free hand.

"Yes; I'll tell you," he said. "Let the fools hunt. They'll never find it. Well? Why not? It is mine. Look. You count along here — do you see — one, eight, six, now press in the key. There is a spring. Press it home and turn. The door opens and there it is. For you, dearest — the jewels are all your own."

As he went on talking rapidly, the curtain moved softly again, and this time Lydia felt that it was no trick of the light or wind, and, rising from her seat, she went softly round to the other side of the bed, took hold of the curtain and swept it aside, to leave Katrine standing there in the faint light shed by the shaded lamp.

"What are you doing here?"

"I came to see if I could help you."

"And glided in like a thief, to hide there, listening to his words. What is it you want to know? Was it to hear him say he loved you?" whispered Lydia, with her face full of scorn.

"I do not understand you."

"You do understand. And it was not for that. You have heard him whisper to you — no — waste upon you loving words enough."

"Really," said Katrine, who had recovered from her temporary confusion, consequent upon the abrupt discovery of her presence. "Surely, my darling little Lydia is not jealous?"

"Jealous? Of you?" said Lydia, scornfully.

"No; I am only sorry that he should have been so blind."

"To your incomparable charms?"

"No; to the character of the beautiful woman — "

"Beautiful?"

"Yes; beautiful woman, whose character — "

"How dare you!" cried Katrine, and she struck the brave girl a sharp blow across the face with her open hand.

"Beautiful as you are corrupt and cruel," said

Lydia, without wincing. "I have not been blind. I have seen your efforts to lead him on — to tempt him into the belief that you loved him, when your sole thought has been of the money that was to be his."

"It is false," cried Katrine.

"It is true. I would not stoop to watch you, but I have seen enough to know you. Go back to your companion — the man who plots and plans with you to gain what you will never find, and do not — "

"Do not what?" cried Katrine, with a malignant look.

Lydia did not reply, but hurried back to where Capel was trying to raise himself up, trembling the while, as he gazed towards the window.

"Look," he said harshly. "There. Don't stop, Katrine, love. There is danger. Don't stop now."

Katrine's face wore a strange waxen hue, as she caught the sick man's hand.

The painful position was brought to an end by the coming of the doctors. Katrine's quick ear was the first to give her warning of their approach, and without another word she softly left the room, stealing away so quietly that when Dr Heston entered, ushering in the great physician, Lydia hardly realised that she was alone.

"Still the same," said Dr Heston. "Humph, yes. My dear madam, will you permit me?"

Lydia looked piteously in his face, losing her self-command the while, as Heston led her from the room, and closed the door, while as she heard it locked on the inside and the sound of the rings passing over the rod, she sank down sobbing on the lion-skin rug, burying her face in her hands, and ignorant of the fact that she was being watched.

## Chapter Twenty Six.
## Capel's Nurses.

"This is your doing, Dr Heston," said Mr Girtle, returning to the dining-room, indignantly, with a card in his hand.

He had been seated at lunch with the doctor, Katrine, and Artis, when Preenham had entered the room, to say that a gentleman wished to see him on important business.

"I dare say it is," said the doctor, "but what have I done?"

"We — the family — had decided to refrain from communication with the police, so as not to draw attention to the peculiar circumstances that have taken place in this house, and I agreed somewhat unwillingly, knowing Mr Capel's feelings as to what has gone before."

"Well," said the doctor, coolly, for the old man seemed to have lost his self-control.

"No, sir, it is not well. Someone has communicated with the police."

He held out the card in his hand, and Katrine winced, while Artis gave her an uneasy look.

"No work of mine, my dear sir; my hands are too full of my patient. Surely he does not say — "

"No, no," said Mr Girtle, hurriedly. "I have not seen him yet. I was so angry that I returned at once. I really beg your pardon, but all this trouble has rather taken me off my balance."

He nodded, and left the room, and Katrine glanced at the doctor.

"Over-work and anxiety, my dear madam," he said. "I shall have to give him a little advice. Now, if you will excuse me, I'll go up-stairs."

"But doctor," cried Katrine; "is Mr Capel really better?"

"It is hardly just to call him better while this delirium continues; but you know what Sir Ronald said."

He went out of the dining-room, and ascended the stairs, leaving Katrine with Artis.

"Where are you going?" said the latter.

"Up to Capel's room."

"What, again?"

"Yes," she said, "again."

"But what have you found out?"

"Wait and see."

"Wait and see? I'm sick of it all," he cried, angrily. "I feel as if I were buried alive, and to make matters worse, you're always away. Look here, I don't like your going and nursing that fellow."

"You stupid boy!" she said softly; and she turned upon him a look that made him catch her in his arms and press his lips to hers.

For a few moments she made no resistance, but seemed to be returning his caress. Then, with an angry wrench, she extricated herself from his grasp.

"How dare you!" she cried.

"How dare? Oh, come, that's good."

"You are acting like a fool!"

She sailed out of the room just as Preenham opened the door, and as he drew back for her to pass, Artis threw himself into a chair, while Katrine slowly ascended the stairs, listening intently to the low murmur of voices in the library.

A few minutes before, the quiet, grave-looking professional nurse had ascended to the sick room from the housekeeper's room, where she had just partaken of her dinner, and found, as she entered, silently, Lydia on her knees by the bedside, with a straight bar of light from the window throwing her into bold relief against the dark curtains.

The nurse advanced softly, and glanced at Capel, who seemed to be sleeping easily, and then lightly touched Lydia on the shoulder.

"Asleep, miss?" she said.

Lydia raised her white face, haggard and livid with sleeplessness and anxiety.

"No," she said softly, as she let herself sink into the low chair at the bed's head. "No, not asleep."

"But you are quite done up, miss," said the nurse. "Now, pray do go and lie down for a few hours. He is better, I'm sure of it. I do know, indeed. I've seen so much of this sort of thing. I was in the French hospitals all through the war."

"But, are you sure?"

"I'm quite certain, miss. Now, you can't go on like this. You must have rest. Take my advice, and go and have a good sleep, and then you can come and watch again."

"But if — "

"If anything happens, miss, I'll call you."

"You promise me?"

"Faithfully, miss. There, trust to me."

Lydia had risen, and she tottered as she took a step or two, when the nurse caught her in her arms, and the poor girl's strength gave way entirely now.

The nurse's confident words that Capel was getting better, robbed her of the last bond of self-control, and, as the woman tenderly supported her, and whispered a few soothing words, Lydia's head went down on the nurse's breast, and she burst into a low, passionate fit of hysterical tears.

"There, you'll be better now," whispered the nurse, as Lydia raised her piteous white face. "Now go and have a few hours' sleep."

Lydia nodded, recovered her self-command, and went to the bed, bent over and gazed earnestly in the patient's face, and then left the room.

"Poor dear!" said the nurse, after a glance at the patient, "how she does love him! Ah, miss, how you made me jump!"

"Did I, nurse?" said Katrine. "I was obliged to

come in gently. How is he?"

"Better, miss, I think."

"That's well. You look very tired, nurse."

"Me, miss? Oh, dear, no."

"But your strength ought to be saved for nights. I can't watch at night — I get too sleepy; but I can now, and I'll take your place."

"Do you really wish it, miss?"

"Yes. Please," said Katrine, firmly; and the woman quietly left the room, to take no walk, but to go up to the chamber set apart for her use, and, from long habit in catching rest when it could be found, she threw herself upon her bed, and was soon breathing heavily — fast asleep.

In the adjoining room lay Lydia, with her eyes closed, hour after hour, but painfully awake. No sleep would come to her weary brain, which seemed to grow more terribly active as the time rolled on. She told herself that her love for Capel was madness. Then hope tortured her with the idea that he might turn to her, while her indignant maiden nature bade her forget him and show more pride. "But he is poor," Hope seemed to say; "his fortune is gone, and you are comparatively wealthy. Wait, and he will love you yet."

There was a hopeful smile dawning upon her lips, as she softly left her room, and went down the stairs, with a feeling of restful content in her breast, and then her heart seemed to stand still, and a horrible feeling of self-reproach attacked her as she felt that she had left her post just as some terrible crisis had been about to happen.

For there, at the door where she had crouched in agony, waiting to know the great physician's verdict, now stood Gerard Artis, gazing in as he held it partly open.

Lydia was as if turned to stone for the moment. Then the reaction came, and she quickly ran to the door, to lay her hand upon Artis's shoulder.

He turned upon her a face distorted with jealous rage, and then his countenance changed, and, indulging in a malicious laugh, he drew on one side, holding the curtain back, and pointed mockingly to the scene within.

## Chapter Twenty Seven.
## An Encounter.

One swift glance, and then, without noticing Artis, Lydia glided into the room.

She had seen her hope crushed, and that she must never dream again of that happy future. She had not slept, but she had left her post, and while she had been absent another had stolen that last hope.

For, after lying sleeping calmly and peacefully for an hour, Capel heaved a long sigh, and at last he opened his eyes, in a quiet, dreamy way, gazing at, but apparently not seeing, Katrine, as she knelt there in the light cast by the window.

Then she saw a look of intelligence come into his face, and he spoke in a quiet and eager, though feeble tone.

"What is it? Why — why am I here? Don't — don't speak. Yes, I know. Oh, Katrine, my love, my love!"

He raised his feeble arms, till they clasped the beautiful neck as she bent down over him, and her head rested upon his pillow, side by side with his; her soft dark hair half hid his pale cheek, and he was whispering feebly his words of gratitude, as Lydia slowly advanced into the room, and, unnoticed by either, she laid her soft, white hand upon Katrine's shoulder, gripping it with a nervous force of which she herself was ignorant.

Katrine started up, flushed, her eyes sparkling

with light, and a look of triumph coming into her face, as she saw who was there.

"Mr Capel's condition will not permit of this excitement," said Lydia, in a cold, harsh voice. "Doctor Heston's orders were that he should be kept quiet."

That afternoon, when Mr Girtle entered the library, he found a plainly-dressed man awaiting him — a man who, save that he gave the idea of having once been a soldier, might have passed for anything, from a publican to an idler whose wife let lodgings, and made it unnecessary for him to toil or spin.

"Morning, sir. You had my card, I see. I've called about the attempt made here the other night."

"Attempt?"

"Yes, sir; the burglary."

"How did you know there was an attempt?"

"Oh, we get to know a little, sir. We're a body of incompetent men that every one abuses, but we find out a few things a year."

"You heard of this, then?"

"Yes, sir, and we were a bit surprised that you didn't communicate with us. Seems strange, sir."

"Strange, yes, my man, but have we not had horrors enough?"

"Yes, sir, but — "

"Well," said Mr Girtle impatiently, "you have heard of it, then? What do you wish to do?"

"See the place, sir. Who is it that nearly killed that poor fellow?"

"How did you know that some one did?"

Mr Girtle's visitor laughed a quiet little laugh.

"Oh, we know, sir. He's horribly bad."

"No; decidedly better."

"No, sir. I was at the hospital this morning, and they don't think he'll live the day. He has let it all out."

"Look here, my man, we are confusing matters," said Mr Girtle.

"Why, you've got a wounded man here?"

"Yes. There, my good fellow, I suppose you must know all, now."

"I suppose we must, sir," said the officer, with a grim smile. "Strange that you should so soon have another trouble here."

"But you have not told me your informant."

"Oh, there's no secret about it, sir. Servant chap went to the bad, and lost his character. Old friend of your footman here who was killed. He picks up with a couple of regular cracksmen, and tells all he knows about the house, and they put up the job."

"Yes, yes. I see. Well?"

"They get in, and catch a Tartar, for this chap was cut down by some one here, and his mates got him away to a wretched hole, where the people were so frightened that they gave information to the police that a man was dying on their premises. Police took him to the hospital, and when he found out how bad he was, he made a clean breast of it all. That's it, sir. Plain as A, B, C."

Mr Girtle sat looking at the officer, curiously.

"Do you think," he said at last, "that these men committed the other robbery?"

The detective's eyes twinkled, but not a muscle moved.

"I should think it about certain, sir."

"Have you got the man's companions?"

"Yes, sir, both of them, safe enough."

"Then as this man confessed one thing, I dare say he will the other. He is dying, you say?"

"Yes, sir, no doubt about it; not so much from the sword cut, as from bad health — drink, and the like."

"Then he must be seen to-day — at once, man. We may get to know from him where they have disposed of the treasure. — Such a large sum."

"Yes, sir," the officer, quietly, taking out a notebook. "Now, don't you think, sir, you being a solicitor, it would have been better to let us do our work, and you do yours?"

"What do you mean, sir?"

"Only this, sir, that here's another thing. You've had a tremendous robbery here before, and we've known nothing about it till this minute, when you let it all out."

Mr Girtle gave his knee an impatient blow.

"Yes, sir, you let it out. When did it happen?"

"At the time of that terrible affair in the house. You remember?"

"Yes, sir, I took a good deal of notice of it at the time, sir; but I had nothing to do with the case. So a lot of money was taken, then?"

Mr Girtle nodded.

"I am not at liberty to say more. Mr Capel would not have the search made."

"If you'll excuse me, sir, I'll give you another look in. Perhaps, to-morrow, you'll let me go over the place."

He went away hurriedly, and straight off to the hospital, where he had a long interview with the sick man, obtaining all the information from him that he could, before compelled by the poor wretch's weakness to cease the inquisition.

"A tremendous big sum, eh?" said the officer, to himself. "I should like to have the finding of that. They might be a bit generous to a man."

# Chapter Twenty Eight.
## Mr Preenham's Visitor.

There was a kind of civil war carried on at the old house over the nursing back of Paul Capel to health. He suffered much, but a strong constitution and youth were fine odds in his favour, and he recovered, after passing the crisis, rapidly and well.

And during these days Lydia suffered a martyrdom, seeing, as she did, how Katrine took advantage of Capel's weakness to tighten his bonds.

The detective came, as he had promised, and saw the room and the window, making notes and a drawing thereof, and then going to the mews at the back, where he satisfied himself as to the means by which access had been obtained.

The evidence of Paul Capel was taken by a magistrate at his bedside, as he was certified as unfit to be moved; and in due time the law meted out its punishment upon the two criminals left; but the detective was not at peace.

The officer, who boasted of the name of Linnett, was a very sleuth-hound in his ways, and he came upon Mr Girtle at all manner of unexpected times while he was waiting for Paul Capel's return to health, and tried to get information from him, without avail.

"Must have been a bit of imagination on the old man's part," said Mr Linnett. "Some of these old fellows — half-cracked, as a rule — believe that they are extremely rich. I don't know, though. Old boy was very rich. Wonderful! What a house! That young chap might very well be satisfied with what he has got."

In this spirit the detective turned his attention to the doctor, approaching him with a bad feeling of weakness, and not being satisfied with the dictum of the divisional surgeon.

"He laughs at it, you see, sir," said Linnett, in the doctor's consulting room; "but I'm bad."

"Yes, yes. I see what is the matter with you, my man," said Heston. "I'll soon set you all right."

"Lor', what humbugs doctors are," said the detective, looking at his prescription, as he went away. "I suppose I must take this stuff, though, before I go and see him again."

"Curious thing, nature," said Heston, as soon as the detective had gone; "that man thinks he's ill, and there's nothing whatever the matter with him. Fancy, brought on from hard thought and work."

The doctor was wiser than the detective thought; but in future visits the latter obtained a good deal of information, among which was the doctor's theory that Ramo, the old Indian servant, had not died entirely from the struggle with Charles Pillar.

It was just about that time that Gerard Artis swore an oath.

That old Mr Girtle took Lydia's hand gently between his, and said tenderly: —

"No, no, my child. You must not go. I am very

old, and if you were to go now, it would be like taking the light out of my life. I know all; I am not blind. But wait."

Lydia shook her head.

"If you love him, my child, wait. It may be to save him, and you would sacrifice yourself to do that."

And that Mr Linnett went out of the area of the great gloomy house, laughing to himself, and casting up his total, as he termed it.

"Ha! ha! ha!" he exclaimed; "only to think of them knocking their heads about here and there, and never so much as getting warm. Detectives are all fools, so the public say. Blind as bats. They want a better class of men."

He treated himself to a thoroughly good cigar, and rolled out the blue clouds of smoke as he strode along, wagging his umbrella behind him.

"Always through all these years running down rogues! What a temptation to a man, to make a change and go the other way. Million and a half o' money, in a shape as could be carried in a small black bag. Why, I could put my hand on it, and go and set up somewhere as a king, and never be found out. Shall I?"

It was quite dark, and Mr Linnett took a pair of handcuffs from his pocket, and tucking his umbrella under his arm, playfully fitted them on his own wrists.

"No," he said; "they wouldn't look well there."

## Chapter Twenty Nine.
## The Party breaks up.

"Dinner over, of course, Preenham?"

"Oh, dear, yes, sir," said that worthy, taking Artis's hat and cane. "Carriage was ordered for half-past seven, and they've gone to the theatre, sir."

"Gone where?"

"Theatre, sir — Haymarket, sir."

"Why, Preenham — "

"It was Mr Girtle, sir, proposed it. Said it would be a pleasant change for everybody. The carriage was ordered, and dinner an hour sooner."

"The sky will fall next," said Artis, with a sneering laugh. "Bring me some coffee in the library, and — no, some brandy and soda and the cigars."

"Yes, sir. Miss D'Enghien's in the drawing-room, sir. Had a bad headache, and didn't go."

"Why didn't you say that at first?" cried Artis; and he went up two stairs at a time, to find Katrine in the act of throwing herself into a chair, and looking flushed and hot.

"You here?" she said, wearily.

"My darling!" he cried. "If I had only known. At last!"

He threw himself at her feet, clasped her waist, and drew her half resisting towards him, while before a minute had elapsed, her arms were resting upon his shoulders, and her eyes were half closed in a dreamy ecstasy, as she yielded to the kisses that covered her face.

Suddenly, with a quick motion, she threw him off.

"Quick — some one," she whispered.

Her ears were sharper than his, and she had heard the dull rattle of the door handle.

"I don't know what to take," she said, in a weary voice; "I suppose it will not be better before morning."

"I have taken the brandy and soda into the library, sir," said Preenham. "Would you like it brought up here?"

"To be sure," he cried. "The very thing for your headache. Bring it up, Preenham."

"You madman!" cried Katrine, angrily. "You take advantage of my weakness for you. Another moment, and we should have been discovered. No, no; keep away."

"Miss is as good as a mile."

"You grow more reckless, every day. We must be careful."

"Careful! I'm sick of being careful."

"Hush!"

The butler entered with a tray and the brandy and soda.

"Open it, sir?"

"Yes. Two. Now try that. Best thing in the world for a bad head."

The old butler withdrew as softly as he had come in, and Katrine took two or three sips from her glass, while Artis tossed his off, and then, setting it down, walked quickly to the door.

Katrine's eyes dilated, and, bending forward, she listened, and then sprang up and glided quickly across from the inner room to meet Artis half-way, and be clasped in his arms.

"What have you done?" she cried.

"Nothing."

"You have fastened the door."

"Nonsense."

"I say you have!"

"Well, suppose I have. What then?"

"You madman! Unfasten the door."

"Not I."

"I tell you that you are mad," she cried, trying to free herself. "Gerard, dear Gerard, be reasonable."

She writhed herself free and ran and turned the bolt back. He followed to refasten it, but she held him.

"Think of the consequences of our being found locked in here."

"Bah! no one will come now till after eleven, and if they did I don't care. Look here," he cried, clasping her to his breast again, "suppose this Arabian Night sort of fortune were found, do you think I am blind? You would marry this Capel."

"Well?"

"I won't have it," he cried.

"Why not?" she whispered, and her creamy arms clasped about his neck. "We are so poor, Gerard, and we must have money to live."

"Yes, but at that cost," he cried, passionately.

"Well, what then? Think! Over a million, which you should share. Gerard — dearest — you will not be so foolish, when I am so near this gigantic prize. He is my complete slave. I can do with him just what I will."

"But — Kate — I believe you would — "

He did not achieve his sentence, but responded passionately to her caresses till he felt her suddenly grow rigid in his arms, and then one arm was snatched from his neck, and, with her hand, she struck him sharply across the face.

"How dare you!" she cried.

Gerard Artis let his hands fall to his side, and Katrine darted to a tall figure in evening dress standing just inside the door, and flung herself at his knees.

"Save me!" she half shrieked, "from the insults of this man."

Paul Capel drew himself aside, and Katrine fell prostrate on the thick carpet, as he gravely opened the door.

The girl sprang to her feet and darted out of the room, while Capel, after watching her for a moment or two, closed the door, turned the bolt, and then threw his crush hat upon a table, his black wrapper over a chair, and tore off his white gloves, changing the ivory-handled malacca cane from hand to hand as he did so.

"Home soon," said Artis, with a sneer, as he slowly walked to the little table, poured out some more brandy, and gulped it down.

"Yes," replied Capel, gravely. "Thank Heaven I did come home soon. I came to spend an hour alone with the woman I loved."

"And you were forestalled," cried Artis. "Here, what are you going to do?"

"Thrash a contemptible scoundrel within an inch of his life," cried Capel; and he made a grasp at Artis's arm.

But the latter eluded him, bounded to the fire-place, and picked up the bright poker.

"Keep off," he cried, "or I'll murder you."

*Cling! Jingle!*

He had struck the glass lustres of the great chandelier, and the fragments fell tinkling down.

*Crack!* A yell of pain! A dull thud!

With a dexterous blow, Capel caught Artis's right hand with the stout cane, numbing his nerves, so that the poker fell. With a second blow, he seemed to hamstring his adversary, who staggered, and would have fallen, but for Capel's hand grasping him by the collar; and then, for two or three minutes, there was a hail of blows falling, and a terrible struggle going on. The light chairs were kicked aside, a table overturned, a vase and several ornaments swept from a cheffonier, and suppressed cries, panting noises and blows, filled the gloomy room, till, after one final stroke with the cane, Capel dashed the helpless, quivering man to the floor, and placed his foot upon his breast.

An hour later, when Preenham went up from a confidential talk with his fellow-servants to admit Mr Girtle and Lydia — back from the theatre — he found the front door open. Had he been half an hour sooner, he would have seen Katrine, fully dressed, supporting Artis down the dark stairs, and out into the darkness of the great square, where they were seen by the light of one of the street lamps to enter a cab, and then they passed out of sight.

Preenham saw nothing, and Mr Girtle and Lydia ascended to the drawing-room, the latter feeling light-hearted and happy, in spite of the evening's disappointment.

The old lawyer uttered a cry of dismay, as he saw the wreck, and that Capel was seated in a low chair, bent down, with his face buried in his hands.

"My dear boy! What is it?" he cried, as Lydia ran to his side, and her soft hand was laid or his.

"Don't touch me, woman," he almost yelled, as he sprang from his chair. "Oh," he said, softly, "it is you?"

He took and kissed her hand, and then left the room.

"Preenham, what does this mean?" cried Mr Girtle, as the butler brought in lights; and they learned the truth.

# Chapter Thirty.
## Where the Treasure lay.

Six months elapsed before Mr Linnett put into execution the project he had had in his mind that night when he playfully tried the handcuffs on his wrists.

He had meant business, as he termed it, the next morning, but on presenting himself at the chief office, one of his superiors sent for him, and announced an important task.

"Extradition, eh, sir? America?"

"Yes. Cross at once; put yourself in communication with the New York police, and then spare no expense. He must be found."

"When shall I start, sir?"

"Now."

Mr Linnett did start *now*, saying to himself as he entered a carriage for Liverpool:

"Well, they didn't set me the job. It was my own doing, and the news will keep."

So it came about that one morning, when he presented himself at the Dark House, he was saluted by Mr Preenham with:

"Why, how *do* you do? We thought we'd quite lost you, Mr Linnett, sir. You look quite brown."

"I've been pretty well all over America since I saw you, Mr Preenham, and now, sir, just go and give them my card and say I want to see them on very particular business."

"Have you found out anything, Mr Linnett?"

"You wait a bit, my dear sir. Just take up the card."

Mr Girtle was in the library with Paul Capel at the time, for the old man had settled down there, treating the younger as if he were a son. He had talked several times of going, but Capel begged him not to leave, and he always stayed.

"Well, Preenham, for me?"

"He said you and master, sir — the gentleman."

"Ah! Linnett. The detective. Will you see him?"

"No," said Capel, sternly. "I don't want that affair opened again."

"But my dear boy — "

"There; very well. Show him up."

The detective came in, smiling, but only to encounter a stern look in return.

"I've called, gentlemen, about that little matter of the notes and jewels that were lost."

"My good fellow," said Capel, angrily, "I will not have that matter taken up again. It is dead."

"Well, sir, the fact is, you wouldn't let me take it up; but I did it on my own account."

"You did?" said Mr Girtle.

"Yes, sir; it took me months piecing together, as

I had to do it all from the outside, without seeing the place. I was sent abroad, and have only just come back. Last night, however, I took out my notes and went into it again, and I think I can say I've found the treasure."

"Found it, man?" cried Capel, interested in spite of himself. "Where? The place was thoroughly well searched."

"Oh! yes, sir, of course."

"Then you know who took it?"

"Yes, sir; that's it."

"Who was it, then?"

"Ah! come, sir, that's better."

"Yes, yes, go on," cried Capel excitedly, and at that moment it was not the treasure that filled his eyes, but the figure of a sweet, gentle girl, who had watched beside his sick bed.

"Well, the fact is, gentlemen, I very soon came to the conclusion that the great treasure had not been stolen."

"Why?" said Mr Girtle.

"No notes were put in circulation that I could find — old notes — and no valuable jewels sold."

"To be sure, yes," said Mr Girtle. "My idea."

"That wasn't worth much, gentlemen; but I felt sure from the beginning that the treasure was taken by someone on the premises."

"Not that couple, I'll swear," said Mr Girtle.

"Nor the servants," said Capel.

"There, sir, it's all in a nutshell," said Linnett, hesitating.

"Stop!" said Mr Girtle. "What terms do you propose for this information?"

"Oh, sir, I wasn't hesitating about that, but because I don't like letting it go now I've found it. It was so much trouble to find the clue, I hardly like parting with it. But here you are, sir, and if I may make terms, I may say I'm only a few pounds out of pocket — ten will cover it — but I should like it if Mr Capel here would give me that Indian knife, that kukri. I've a fancy for saving up that sort of article."

"Take the horrible thing and welcome," said Capel impatiently.

"Well, gentlemen, I pieced together all that was published, with Doctor Heston's notions, the servants' knowledge, and my own ideas."

"Well?"

"Well, gentlemen, it was that old Indian servant who took the treasure."

"Impossible!"

"Not a bit. He had the keys — he knew how to use them."

"He was as honest as the day," cried Mr Girtle.

"Exactly, sir, that's just it. Honesty made him take it."

"Absurd?" said Capel.

"Not a bit, sir, excuse me. He knew that fellow Pillar, the footman, meant it. You know he had a fight with him at the door."

"Well, granted," said Capel.

"He watched, sir, night and day, and wouldn't leave the place, and at last, when — "

"I know," said Capel, "those Italians."

"Now, you shouldn't take away people's character, sir," said the detective reproachfully. "It was that Indian. He wasn't satisfied that the secret place was safe. He was sure it would be broken open, and so that night, or the one before, he took the treasure out, and put it where he felt certain that no one would look for it."

"And where was that?" cried Capel.

The detective smiled.

"As I said, gentlemen, where no one would look for it."

"And that was?"

"In the dead man's own charge, sirs. *In the coffin.*"

Capel and Mr Girtle sank back in their chairs.

"And if you open that vault, gentlemen, and the iron tomb, and the steel chest, you'll find it safe and sound."

"There's one more thing, sir, I should like to

say, and that is about that old Indian servant. He was struck down, no doubt, or fainted after he had killed the footman, defending the treasure. I can't quite say what happened then, but it looks to me as if some one came upon the old fellow when he was lying helpless — some one who also meant to steal that treasure — and that he, or she, or whoever it was, chloroformed the old man to death. I had it on the doctor's authority that he did not die of his wounds; but this is only theory. I can't say."

It was a theory that sent a chill through Paul Capel, and he dared not put his thoughts about the fair Creole into shape.

All proved about the treasure precisely as Mr Linnett had said, for when, with much compunction, the various caskets were opened once again, there lay the two cases beneath the cloth-of-gold robe, safely in the keeping of the dead man, whereat, and for other reasons, Mr Linnett much rejoiced.

Later on, old Mr Girtle had his wish, that of giving Lydia away to the man she loved — one who often afterwards told her he wondered how he could have been so blind — blind, he said, as the old place, which was kept, in accordance with the Colonel's last commands, closed in front, but bright and gay behind, while Paul Capel used to say, "It is astonishing how much human sunshine can be got into a Dark House."

www.ingramcontent.com/pod-product-compliance
Lightning Source LLC
Chambersburg PA
CBHW020230030726
47497CB00009B/3030